"That's quite a line, Mr. Tabor.

"Does it usually get results?" Brooke asked coolly.

"You don't trust me at all, do you?" he said. "I don't play games. I really don't. I deal with facts in my work, and it carries over to my social life. So you see, Brooke, if I say I find you attractive and nice to be with, I mean it. That's about as honest as I can get."

Honest. The word seemed to roar in Brooke's ears as she gazed into the depths of Chance's eyes.

"Who was he?" Chance asked quietly.

"Pardon me?"

"The man who made you so wary, so untrusting? Do you think it's fair to blame all men for something one did?" He looked at her steadily, a gentle expression on his face.

"I don't! Chance, you don't understand."

"Try me."

Dear Reader,

Welcome to Silhouette! Our goal is to give you hours of unbeatable reading pleasure, and we hope you'll enjoy each month's six new Silhouette Desires. These sensual, provocative love stories are both believable and compelling—sometimes they're poignant, sometimes humorous, but always enjoyable.

Indulge yourself. Experience all the passion and excitement of falling in love along with our heroine as she meets the irresistible man of her dreams and together they overcome all obstacles in the path to a happy ending.

If this is your first Desire, I hope it'll be the first of many. If you're already a Silhouette Desire reader, thanks for your support! Look for some of your favorite authors in the coming months: Stephanie James, Diana Palmer, Dixie Browning, Ann Major and Doreen Owens Malek, to name just a few.

Happy reading!

Isabel Swift
Senior Editor

SDRL-7/85

ROBIN ELLIOTT
Brooke's Chance

Silhouette Desire

Published by Silhouette Books New York

America's Publisher of Contemporary Romance

SILHOUETTE BOOKS
300 East 42nd St., New York, N.Y. 10017

Copyright © 1986 by Joan Elliott Pickart

ISBN: 0-373-05323-1

First Silhouette Books printing December 1986

Books by Robin Elliott

Silhouette Desire

Call It Love #213
To Have It All #237
Picture of Love #261
Pennies in the Fountain #275
Dawn's Gift #303
Brooke's Chance #323

ROBIN ELLIOTT

lives in Arizona with her husband and three daughters. Formerly employed in a high school library, she is now devoting her time to writing romance novels. She also writes under her own name, Joan Elliott Pickart.

For my editor, Tara Hughes,
whose enthusiasm is infectious.
Thank you.

One

No! Absolutely not,'' Brooke Bradley said adamantly. "I won't do it.''

"Have you no honor?''

"Julie, take pity on me!''

"You lost the bet fair and square. The Rams beat the Cowboys by a field goal, and you have to pay up.''

"This is ridiculous,'' Brooke said. "I'm twenty-three years old, for Pete's sake. I can't go sit on that Santa Claus's lap. There're a dozen kids in that line, and not one of them is over four. Julie, I'm your best friend. Don't do this to me!''

"Did I or did I not stand on the corner last week and sing 'Joy to the World' at the top of my lungs because Shirley had a baby boy instead of a girl?''

"So? A man gave you a quarter and said you had a nice voice.''

"March!''

Brooke's gaze swept over the milling crowds in the large mall that was decorated for the holiday season. Christmas music could be heard above the din of voices, and the mood was festive. And there in the direct line of traffic, for all to see, was Santa Claus. He sat on his throne and received the children who were led to his lap by a girl dressed in a skimpy elf outfit. An arched sign read Welcome to the North Pole, and Brooke had the irrational thought that traveling to the actual icy location would be a marvelous idea.

"Beebee," Julie said firmly, "go!"

"Oh, brother," Brooke said. "Well, hold my coat."

"Why?"

"That's an old man up there who's used to little kids plunking on his lap. I weigh a hundred and five pounds. I might break his leg or something."

"You're a real humanitarian." Julie giggled. "Okay, give me your stuff."

Brooke shrugged out of her coat and handed it to Julie, along with her purse and packages. Brooke frowned as she straightened her bulky knit red sweater and smoothed it over the waistband of her jeans. Dark brown eyes flickered over the line of children waiting to visit the jolly old Santa, and she absently fluffed her short, dark curls around her face. Small-boned and petite, Brooke now felt like an Amazon, and she glowered at Julie before making her way to the end of the line.

"Ask for something great," Julie called.

Brooke groaned.

"Hi," Brooke said to the little girl in front of her. "How's life? If anyone asks, I'm your mother."

"I can't speak to strangers."

"Sorry. I won't say another word."

Brooke studied her fingernails, the decorations hanging overhead, hummed along with the piped-in carols and totally ignored Julie Mason.

"Yoo-hoo, Beebee," Julie sang out. "You're next, sweetheart. Remember to say please when you ask for your presents."

"I'll kill her," Brooke muttered.

The girl in the elf suit turned to Brooke and hesitated. "Where's your kid, lady?" she asked.

"I'm his proxy," Brooke said. "He has the measles."

"Well, I guess it's okay, but . . ."

"Don't worry about a thing," Brooke said, marching past her and across the carpeted expanse. She stomped up the three steps and planted herself in front of Santa Claus.

"I . . ."she started.

"Ho ho ho," he boomed, the sound rumbling from the depths of his well-padded, red velvet stomach.

"Listen up, Santa. Julie always talks me into these insane bets, and the Cowboys were fumble fingers and lost so here I am, and the quicker we get this over with, the better. Oh, Lord!" Brooke shrieked, as large hands grasped her around the waist and deposited her squarely on a very firm leg.

"Ho ho ho," Santa bellowed.

"Would you knock that off? I, um . . ."

Brooke stopped speaking as she found herself staring into the bluest eyes she'd ever seen. Fringed in dark lashes, the sapphire pools were dancing with merriment. Heavy white cotton eyebrows came together over a straight, tanned nose, and his bronzed cheeks were edged by a thick white beard. Her glance slid to soft lips beneath a bushy cotton mustache and then returned to gaze into the blue eyes. The eyelid of one lowered slowly and winked at her.

"You're not an old man," she said, suddenly aware of the heat from the Santa's large hands that was evident even through her sweater.

"Ho ho ho," he said and smiled at her, revealing straight white teeth. "Are you any good?" he asked, his voice rich and deep. "No, that's not right. I'm supposed to say, 'Have you been a good girl?' Well?"

"I'm wonderful," Brooke said. "Let me go."

"But you haven't told me what you want for Christmas," he said, the fingers of one hand moving over to draw lazy circles on her back.

"Stop that," Brooke whispered.

"What," he said quietly, his voice seeming to drop an octave, "do you . . . want me . . . to give you?"

Brooke couldn't breathe. The air swished from her lungs, and her heart beat a wild cadence. Santa was looking at her steadily, all amusement having vanished from the blue eyes that held her mesmerized, unable to move. He had a fever, poor baby, she thought wildly. The heat from his hands and the solid leg that she was perched on was radiating through her clothing and sending funny, tingling sensations throughout her entire body.

"A . . . Saint Bernard," she said breathlessly.

"What?"

"A dog. A Saint Bernard. Well, it was nice chatting with you. See ya."

"But you haven't told me your name. How will I know where to deliver the dog?"

"Ask your elves. Surely you've computerized your system by now."

"I'll see you when you're sleeping."

"I beg your pardon?"

"So," he said, chuckling, the throaty sound having a disconcerting effect on Brooke's nervous system, "be good, for goodness' sake. Or however the saying goes. Goodbye for now."

"Bye...Santa," Brooke said, not moving as she was once again held fast by the man's compelling blue eyes. "You smell like mothballs."

"It's the suit. They must have had it stuffed away since last year."

"Santa," the skimpily clad elf said, "the kids are getting impatient."

"Oh!" Brooke said, jumping to her feet. "Yes! Well, goodbye."

"See you soon," Santa said, winking at her again.

"Ho ho ho," Brooke said, hurrying down the steps and joining her roommate. "Julie, come on," she said a moment later. "Let's get out of here."

"Just a sec," Julie said. "I have to get my change."

"For what?"

"The picture I'm having mailed of you sitting on Santa's lap."

"Oh, good Lord," Brooke said.

Brooke walked away and then turned to wait for Julie, only then allowing herself the luxury of a deep, steadying breath. They hadn't made Santas like that when *she* was a kid! Never in her life had she seen such gorgeous blue eyes. But what would he look like without the fake beard and those silly eyebrows? What she had seen of his face was deeply tanned. Did he ski? Oh, who cared!

"All set," Julie said. "Here's your coat."

"I need a hot fudge sundae."

"You're *that* upset? Why? You looked so cute on that old geezer's lap. What did you ask him to bring you?"

"A Saint Bernard."

"You're kidding." Julie laughed. "How dumb."

"I was rather shook up at the time. Julie, that Santa was *not* old."

"Oh?" Julie glanced quizzically at her friend as they left the department store.

"No. I need my sundae," Brooke said, pulling open the door to an ice-cream parlor.

Several heads turned as the two young women made their way across the room and sat in a booth. Brooke, with her petite figure and large dark eyes, soft brown curls and lovely smile often was the recipient of such descriptions as cute, fresh and wholesome, which caused her to wrinkle her nose in disgust.

Julie Mason was five foot ten in her stockinged feet and had skin the color of cocoa. She wore her hair in a short Afro cut, which accentuated her high cheekbones and ebony eyes. She was reed slim, and her fervent wish was to become a model. Julie had perfected a sophisticated air and a slightly bored expression that she evoked at will, and she had a fun-loving, adventuresome nature. She was constantly conning Brooke into making bets with outrageous penalties for the loser.

The pair had met while in business school, had become instant friends and had shared an apartment for the past three years. It had been Julie who had seen Brooke through the heartbreak of a broken engagement two years previously.

"Hot fudge sundae, please," Brooke said to the waitress.

"Ice water," Julie said. "So, how old was Saint Nick?"

"Young."

"Fourteen? Eighteen? What?"

"I don't know for sure. He had all those whiskers covering his face. Thirty, maybe."

"Really?" Julie said, leaning forward. "Was he beautiful?"

"Who knows? I couldn't really see his face, but, Julie, the man's eyes were enough to make me weep. Blue as sapphires."

"And you asked him for a Saint Bernard? You should have asked for his body, gift wrapped and delivered on Christmas Eve. What's his name?"

"Santa Claus."

"You were sitting on a hunk of stuff's lap and you didn't find out his name? You're hopeless. I swear, you really are. Did you tell him yours?"

"Nope."

"What am I going to do with you?"

"Hey, maybe he's really gross under all that beard, and he could be fat. You know, that was *him* in that suit. Cancel that. His leg was very... taut."

"Taut?"

"And warm. Oh, forget it."

"Santa Claus had a taut, warm leg?" Julie said, bursting into laughter. "What about his hands? I saw him haul you onto his lap."

"Big, strong and *very* warm. I think he had a fever."

"Blue eyes, huh?"

"Like you wouldn't believe," Brooke said.

"Want to bet they were colored contacts?"

"I am never betting anything with you again, Julie. You're going to get me thrown into jail one of these days."

"Don't you at least want to know his name?"

"No! Here's my ice cream. Don't disturb me while I'm calming my nerves."

Julie suppressed her laughter and waited patiently for Brooke to consume the dessert. The pair then headed out the door and to the mall exit.

The Denver night was clear and cold with snow flurries swirling through the air. Christmas decorations were in abundance, and the gaily lit stores and decorated windows helped create some of the preholiday excitement that seemed to crackle in the air.

"I love this time of year," Julie said.

"So you've said at least three times a day." Brooke laughed. "You're worse than a little kid and there're still three weeks until Christmas."

"Oh? At least *I* didn't sit on Santa's lap, my dear. I can hardly wait to tell Gran about *this* one."

Santa's lap, Brooke thought absently. And a very nice lap it had been. What did the rest of that tanned face look like? Colored contacts? No, she wanted his eyes to really be that blue, that clear and sparkling. When he had gazed at her, she had literally melted, had been unable to move. What silliness, she scolded herself. He was simply a man in a red suit.

The snow was falling more heavily by the time the two women arrived at their apartment building. They stuck out their tongues to catch the frosty flakes and then dashed inside to ride the elevator to the sixth floor. Their apartment was a two-bedroom unit with a bath, a good-sized living room and a small kitchen. It had come furnished, and Brooke and Julie had added their personal touches with plants, bright throw pillows and a bookcase filled to overflowing with a variety of reading material.

"I've got to do my exercises," Julie said, heading for her bedroom. "There's the phone. Will you get it?"

"Yep," Brooke said, grabbing the receiver. "Hello?"

"Brooke Bradley, please."

"Speaking."

"I forgot to ask you if you've been naughty or nice."

"Santa Claus?" Brooke said, her eyes widening as she sank onto the sofa.

"The same. Now, are you naughty or nice?"

"How did you get my number? And my name, for that matter."

"Easy. Your friend filled out a card addressed to you to have the picture sent. The clerk remembered her and said the name on the form was the woman in the photograph. You. Brooke Bradley."

"You're very resourceful," Brooke said, extremely glad that he could not see the smile on her face. "Have you finished playing Santa?"

"Nope, I'm on my break. I have to get back in a couple of minutes. So, you bet on Dallas, huh? Not bright, but I'm glad you did. You sure perked up my evening, Brooke Bradley. Here comes my elf to collect me. Gotta go. I'll talk to you soon."

"But—"

"See ya. Oh, my name is Chance Tabor. Night, Brooke."

"Good night," she said to the dial tone, shaking her head slightly. So, his name was Chance. Chance Tabor with the beautiful blue eyes and sexy, sexy voice. He'd gone to all that fuss to get her name? Fancy that. But why was she thrilled? She didn't even know Chance Tabor, and now he had her address as well. He could be weird, for all she knew. No, Santas weren't weird. Lord, he was a man, not a fantasy! He was *definitely* a man. But who was he, and what did he look like without the phony beard? And why was she spending so much time wondering about him? Enough was enough.

When Julie emerged from the bedroom a half hour later clad in a pink leotard and tights, Brooke was still sitting on the sofa.

"Cold?" Julie said.

"What?"

"You haven't taken off your coat."

"Oh," Brooke said, "I forgot."

"Who was on the phone?"

"Phone?"

"Beebee, what is wrong with you? Who called?"

"Santa Claus."

"Santa? Really? Really? The blue-eyed Santa? How did he know your name?"

"He got it off that card you filled out for the picture. His name is Chance Tabor."

"Oh, Lord, what a gorgeous name. It's so...macho. He should go into politics. Can you picture campaign signs saying Take a Chance with Chance? Marvelous. What did he say?"

"Not much. His elf came to get him. He asked whether I was naughty or nice."

"What?"

"Santas have to investigate those things," Brooke said, bursting into laughter. "Great. I'm getting hysterical. Do you realize that a man I don't even know has my address and phone number? This is terrible."

"Now wait a minute," Julie said, sitting Indian-style on the floor. "Let's analyze this. They don't let just anyone play Santa. He'd have to have references saying he's an upstanding citizen and worthy of the privilege. Right? And not only that, we know he's intelligent because look how easily he discovered your name. And you're not total strangers because you did sit on his lap. That's more than you do with a guy you've been out with six times."

"So?"

"So there's no problem. Except..."

"Except what?"

"Well, you really don't know what he looks like. Would you be turned off if he was bald? Plus, why would an intelligent, thirty-year-old man have to resort to playing Santa to pay the rent? Unless, of course, he has six kids or..."

"He's married?"

"Did he look married?"

"Julie, you are giving me the crazies!"

"Let's assume he's single. Broke, but single. I know! Look him up in the phone book and see what area of town he lives in."

"Skid row is unlisted." Brooke frowned, adding, "This is dumb."

"It is not!" Julie said, walking to the closet to get the telephone book and flipping through it. "Nothing. Darn."

"He can't afford a phone, remember? Did I mention he had a tan?"

"Oh, good, more clues. Well, that means skiing in Aspen or wherever, or a vacation in the sun and surf, which is pretty tough to do without money, or he just moved here. Yes, that's it. He's new in town. Hence the Santa suit until he can find a job. I'll call the operator and see if she has an address and phone number."

"They don't give out addresses."

"Can't hurt to ask," Julie said, picking up the receiver. "Merry Christmas, Operator," she said cheerfully, then continued with her request.

Brooke tuned out Julie's chatter and scowled. Why did she always go along with Julie's nonsense? she thought. Brooke didn't care diddly about Chance Tabor. Well, maybe she was a little curious but . . .

"Interesting," Julie said, tapping her chin with her fingertip as she hung up the receiver. "There's no residence telephone for a Chance Tabor. The closest she came was Tabor Computer Corporation, and it's not new. Let's see," Julie said, opening the telephone book again. "Yep, here it is in the business section. He's in the Meredith Building. Swanky."

"You don't know that it's Chance. In fact, it's dumb to think it is. Why would the owner of a computer corporation moonlight as a Santa Claus?"

"Beats me."

"Enough of this. I'm going to take a bubble bath."

"I'm going to yank on my jeans and dash over to Gran's," Julie said. "I can hardly wait to tell her about you and Señor Claus, Beebee."

"Spare me."

Gran was a plump woman in her sixties who lived across the hall from Brooke and Julie and who fussed over them as though they were her granddaughters. Widowed for twenty years, Virginia Jones, lovingly called Gran by the two young women, had no children and blessed the day that Brooke and Julie had moved into the building.

Brooke rarely saw her father, who had raised her alone since his wife's death when Brooke was six. Mac Bradley traveled extensively as a correspondent for a Denver newspaper and sent Brooke hastily scribbled postcards from around the world. Julie's parents and three brothers lived in California.

Brooke ran a tubful of hot water and sprinkled it with lemon-scented bath crystals. After dropping her clothes into the hamper, she sank into the bubbly water up to her chin and closed her eyes. When the image of a blue-eyed Santa Claus popped into her mind, she opened her eyes again and frowned.

"Chance Tabor," she said, "stay away from me! Go pester Rudolph."

The next morning Denver was a marshmallow fairyland. Snow had fallen steadily throughout the night, and the weatherman promised more for the day. Schools were closed and snowplows worked slowly, trying to clear the main streets to allow the citizens to get work.

Brooke and Julie elected to ride the bus rather than maneuver their compact cars through the hazardous traffic and weather conditions, and they parted outside the building. Brooke would head downtown to the attorney's office where she was a secretary, and Julie would go in the opposite direction to her position as a bookkeeper for a construction company.

Brooke usually enjoyed the beauty of the snow, the cold invigorating air, but not today. She was tired. She had not slept well, and it was Chance Tabor's fault. During the night he had crept into her dreams in his Santa Claus suit, smiling at her, his blue eyes sparkling. Brooke woke often, punched her pillow and dozed, only to have a deep voice saying "ho ho ho" creep into her subconscious and jar her awake once again.

Brooke stepped off the bus a block from where she worked and bent her head against the biting wind. She had dressed in brown slacks, a cable-knit tan sweater, a heavy coat and her boots, and she was still freezing.

"Ho ho ho, Merry Christmas!" a voice boomed.

"Aaak!" Brooke screamed.

"Hey, lady, don't freak out," a small, thin Santa said. "This is for charity, you know."

Brooke mumbled her apologies and searched in her purse for a quarter to plunk in the miniature Santa's container.

Chance Tabor was definitely getting on her nerves.

The day was long and quiet since Brooke's boss was handling a court case and called in only once to check on his messages. Brooke caught up on her filing, answered the telephone and frowned a great deal. She was, she realized, playing tug-of-war in her head. One part of her mind fervently wished that Chance Tabor would drop off the face of the earth. But the other section of her brain? There were the questions. What did Chance really look like? Why had he performed like Magnum to obtain her name? And, *and*... would she ever hear from him again?

"Now if I were Julie..." Brooke said in the late afternoon. Julie would do something nutty like call Tabor Computer Corporation and find out if that was Chance's company. That was ridiculous because computer wizards did not need part-time jobs that required dressing up like Santa. But would that stop Julie? She'd pick up the phone and dial the number. So that's exactly what Brooke decided to do.

"Tabor Computer Corporation," a woman said.

"What?" Brooke said, staring at the receiver. Oh, Lord, she had done it. She'd actually done it!

"Tabor Com—"

"Yes! I, um, I am doing an article on the various computer firms in Denver, and I want to be sure I have spelled Mr. Tabor's name correctly."

"It's T—A—"

"Yes, I have that. I was more concerned about his first name," Brooke said, wishing that her heart would stop racing.

"It's Chance. Chance Tabor."

"Are you sure?" Brooke whispered. "Of course you are, you work there. He's . . . about sixty, right?"

"I'm sorry, dear, but I'm really not allowed to give out personal information over the phone. Mr. Tabor was interviewed for the Dynamos of Denver column in the newspaper. The article appeared about two weeks ago and should contain all the data you need. Any other questions?"

What does he look like? Brooke screamed silently. "No," she said. "Thank you so much for your help." *I'm a genius,* Brooke thought merrily. Oh, Julie will be so proud. All Brooke had to do was go to the library and find the back issue of the paper. Dynamos of Denver? Heavens. But why was Chance moonlighting as a Santa? And what did he want with her?

When Brooke left the office, the snow was falling heavily, and she was chilled to the bone by the time she'd trudged the four blocks to the library. She was directed to a section against the wall where the newspapers were suspended on thin metal rods. Hardly breathing, she found the sought-after issue, instantly disappointed that the article did not contain a picture of Chance. She scanned the paragraph quickly, digesting the facts that Chance Tabor was thirty-one, single and considered an up-and-coming genius in the computer field. He was, in short, a Dynamo of Denver, and the Tabor Computer Corporation was on its way to the top!

"It has Santa Claus at the helm," Brooke said dramatically, then left the library to shiver her way to the bus stop. Julie was being picked up at work by a date, and Brooke would have the apartment to herself for a long, hot bath and a quiet evening with a thick novel.

Brooke was asked out frequently by the young men of Denver, but she chose her escorts carefully, seeing more than once only those who did not try to hustle her into bed. She had given her heart and with it her body to the wrong man and was now wary of her own judgment. She didn't mistrust men in general or dislike them, but she questioned her own ability to separate the good guys from the bad. She had the flaw, not them, and was cautious in her relationships.

Julie had given endless speeches about Chuck Finley having been a smooth-talking con artist who could have sold oil to the Arabs. But Brooke blamed herself for not realizing that Chuck was insincere, his promise of marriage and commitment phony and his ongoing excuses for working late and breaking their dates fishy. She had caught him with his secretary on the couch in his office, and her world had come to a screeching halt.

Julie had held Brooke while Brooke had cried and wailed, ranted and raved. She was so stupid, Brooke had moaned. So gullible, naive and...dumb! It wasn't Chuck's fault! It was hers for not having the brains to see through his scam. She needed a keeper, not a lover, and it would be a cold day in hot places before she trusted her judgment about men again.

Julie pleaded the case from the other side, calling Chuck Finley every name in the book, but Brooke had remained firm. Men were nifty creatures, but Brooke Bradley was not getting seriously involved with another one. With her luck she'd fall head over heels in love with a Mafia hit man who had passed himself off as a Sunday school teacher! She wasn't bitter. She was simply being realistic.

To Brooke, Chuck's defection was the crowning blow in a long list of poor judgments regarding the male species. In high school she had been aglow when suddenly sought after by a popular senior. She had adored her Jeffery, had even written his name in indelible ink all over her tennis shoes. But Jeffery's career goal had been to be a reporter, and the attention he paid to Brooke was nothing more than a ploy to attempt to obtain a job on the paper through his connection with Mac Bradley, her father.

During the first year of business school, Brooke had met Henry, a quiet young man in one of her classes. On their first date Henry had taken Brooke home to meet his parents and had found constant excuses to drop in on them with Brooke in tow during the following weeks. Henry had never advanced past the hand-holding stage with Brooke, and she had given serious thought to instigating their first kiss.

Then one night, in a rush of words, Henry had confessed that he was deeply in love with an artist named Richard and had been using Brooke as a smoke screen to divert his parents' growing suspicions. He was leaving town with Richard, Henry had said, then had hurried out the door, leaving Brooke staring after him with her mouth open.

Chuck Finley was the capper. Brooke Bradley had had enough!

Brooke stepped off the elevator and hurried down the hall, searching in her purse for her key. She was freezing and the thought of a bubble bath was holding more and more appeal by the minute. A note taped to the door from the manager said that a package had been delivered to Brooke and that Gran was holding it. Brooke shivered as she knocked on Gran's door and smiled when the older woman answered.

"Hello, Beebee," Gran said. "You look frozen. Come in."

"No, I've got to get out of these things. I just came for my package. My father has never been early for Christmas before."

"It's not from your father. It was sent by special messenger from right here in Denver. I'll get it."

"But who else would be sending me something?"

"Here," Gran said, handing Brooke a gaily wrapped package with a large green bow.

"There must be some mistake," Brooke said.

"Open it, silly girl, and see what it is."

Brooke tore away the paper and gasped as she withdrew the book inside.

"Oh, my heavens!" she said. "*How To Train Your Saint Bernard.* I can't believe this. It has to be from him."

"Him who?"

"Santa Claus. I mean, Chance. Good grief, he's crazy. There's no card, but I just know it's from Chance. Why would he do this? I don't even know him."

"Ahhh, the blue-eyed Santa. Julie told me all about it. I laughed so hard I got the hiccups. It would seem you've interested Mr. Claus. You say his name is Chance?"

"Yes, Chance Tabor."

"Sexy name."

"Oh, really?" Brooke laughed. "You want sexy? You should see those eyes, hear that voice. Now I tell you, Gran, that all adds up to sexy. What I can't figure out is ... Oh, forget it. I'm turning into an icicle. I'll see you later."

The telephone was ringing when Brooke entered the apartment, and she answered it absently, her gaze riveted on the book in her hand.

"'Lo," she said.

"Ho ho ho!"

"Chance?"

"Yep. Did you get the book?"

"Yes, but why did you send me this?"

"We Santas have a responsibility. I can't deliver a Saint Bernard to someone who doesn't know how to care for it."

"But I really don't want a—"

"You study that book so you'll be eligible to be that dog's mother. There will be a written exam, of course. Have you had dinner?"

"Well, no, I just got home."

"Great. Suppose I pick you up in an hour and we'll go out for something. It's a great night. Denver looks like a Christmas card. It's too pretty to stay in. What do you say?"

"Chance, I hardly even know you."

"Want me to bring my elf along for a chaperon?"

"No, thanks," she said with a laugh. "All right, one hour."

"Terrific."

"But don't you have to be Santa at the mall?"

"Nope. Dress warm. It's nippy out. Bye, Brooke. Brooke. That is such a pretty name. Fits you perfectly. See ya soon."

"Yes, all right," Brooke said, hanging up the receiver as the dial tone hummed. Oh, she was nuts! Totally bonkers! She couldn't go out with Chance Tabor! Why not? Because he was a stranger. Well, not exactly. But still... "And I'm still freezing," she said, marching into the bedroom.

Brooke showered and shampooed her hair, then blow-dried the soft curls into a halo around her head with wisps fanning onto her cheeks. She dressed in dark blue slacks and a blue patterned ski sweater, then applied light lip gloss.

She was nervous, she knew it, and sank onto the sofa with a dejected sigh. Going out with Chance was totally unlike her; it did not fit her mode of conduct. But then, being rendered speechless by piercing blue eyes was rather off-the-wall, too, as was having a man follow her into her dreams. Actually, this was a good idea. She had met Chance under rather bizarre circumstances, and her imagination had taken over. They would spend a perfectly normal evening together and bring things back to their proper perspective. Very good.

When the knock sounded at the door exactly one hour after Chance had called, Brooke sat bolt upright on the sofa and decided to ignore it. Then she took a deep breath, practiced her smile and went to answer the summons.

Two

Chance Tabor.

He was the best-looking man that Brooke had ever seen, and her smile slid right off her lips as she gazed up into his blue eyes. His hair was dark, thick, wavy and sprinkled with snow. Beneath the white cotton eyebrows had been ebony ones, and the false beard had concealed the tanned, rugged planes of his jaw and a square chin that had just the hint of a dimple.

Chance was tall, and his shoulders were wide in the sheepskin jacket he wore. He towered above Brooke, and neither spoke for a moment as their eyes met and held.

"Hello," Chance finally said.

"Hello. Please come in."

"Nice apartment," Chance said as Brooke closed the door behind him. "I guess it's big enough for a Saint Bernard."

"Oh, I really don't want a dog."

"Someone else lives here, too," Chance said, stopping in front of the bookcase.

"Yes, Julie, my roommate."

"That attractive black woman with you at the mall?"

"Yes."

"She looks like a model."

"She'd love to be one, but how did you know I had a roommate?"

"The books. A lot of them have the corners turned down on the pages and the others don't. That indicates two different people are reading them."

"Julie bends the corners," Brooke said, frowning slightly. Goodness, she thought, he should moonlight as a detective instead of a Santa Claus.

"Ready to go?" Chance said, turning and smiling at her.

And what a smile it was. It seemed to spread over his face and end with a sparkle in the blue pools of his eyes. Those eyes. They did funny things to the rate of Brooke's heartbeat and made her momentarily forget where and who she was. Chance Tabor virtually oozed a masculine sensuality by doing nothing more than standing there.

"Yes," Brooke said shakily, reaching for her coat and purse off the sofa.

"Do you like Italian food?"

"Sure."

"Great. Let's go. Is your hair naturally curly?"

"Yes. Why?"

"I like to know little details about people, that's all."

"Fair enough. Okay, are your eyes really that blue, or do you wear contacts?"

Chance whooped in delight and grinned.

"No contacts, I swear."

"Figures. I never bet Julie on the stuff I could have won."

"Like the Dallas Cowboys?"

"Those bums." Brooke smiled. "They clobbered every-one for three weeks straight, but when I'm betting on them? Ugh."

"I'm sending them a fan letter. They were the cause of Brooke Bradley ending up on my lap."

In the elevator Brooke caught the scent of Chance's af-ter-shave and approved of its fresh, woodsy aroma. Some-how she just knew that, when he took off his jacket, there would be a sweater beneath stretched to capacity across a broad chest and wide shoulders. There would be no excess weight on Chance Tabor.

The words *taut* and *warm* came to Brooke's mind as she recalled how she had described to Julie the strong leg she had perched on. Her glance fell to below the hem of Chance's jacket to see dark cords that did, indeed, pull tightly across the bunching muscles in his thighs. She cleared her throat as a tingling sensation danced up her spine, and she concentrated on the blinking lights on the elevator panel.

"Why aren't you being Santa at the mall tonight?" Brooke asked as they walked across the lobby.

"It was a one-night stand." He chuckled. "I've been re-placed."

He'd been fired? Brooke thought wildly. He wasn't trustworthy enough to be a Santa Claus? Oh, dear heaven, what was she doing with this man? No, now wait a minute. People didn't fire Dynamos of Denver!

Outside the air was biting cold, and Brooke sank onto the seat of the plush automobile that Chance led her to, wel-coming its warmth. Chance turned the key in the ignition and edged into the surging traffic.

"You're lucky I was on duty last night," Chance said, a smile on his handsome face. "If you'd landed on my grandfather's lap, he'd probably have kept you there for hours."

"Your grandfather?"

"Yeah, he volunteers to play Santa every year, but he was afraid he was catching a cold and didn't want to be around the kids so I filled in for him. My grandfather is a swinger from the word go. He's a neat old guy."

Darn it, Brooke thought, was there really a grandfather? It sounded reasonable but . . .

"Now, then," Chance said, "let's see where we stand."

"Pardon me?"

"I'm adding up my info. You're Brooke Bradley and you're about twenty-one—"

"Twenty-three."

"Check. You're a lousy gambler but a good sport about paying up when you lose. You have an attractive roommate named Julie who demolishes books, and you like dogs, Saint Bernards in particular."

"I've never met a Saint Bernard," Brooke said, laughing.

"Well, smile when you do because they probably weigh more than you do. I'm guessing that your work entails typing because your fingernails are short. You like lemon-scented soap, and you have a habit of playing with those soft curls on your right cheek. You left the light on in your apartment, which means you're basically cautious. You are also very, very pretty."

Brooke blinked once slowly and closed her mouth, which had dropped open during Chance's dissertation.

"You sound like a computer printout," she said.

"I am," he said, grinning at her as they stopped at a red light. "Tabor Computer Corporation, that's me. I love those little machines. My mind works a lot like that. I gather details as I go and then compute them."

"Don't you get tired of being so alert?"

"Nope. I have found, however, that it does get on some people's nerves. If I bother you, let me know. My grandfather likes me, but my parents can stand a half hour max in my company. I really bug them. My mother is convinced I can read her mind and she has a fit. Oh, well.''

"You really have a grandfather who plays Santa Claus?"

"Well, yeah, I told you that. Didn't you believe me? Well, why should you? You don't really know me. Ask me some questions so you'll feel more comfortable. You're probably used to going out with guys you were introduced to by mutual friends.''

"How did you know that?"

"You're cautious, remember? Would it be easier if I just told you about myself?"

"Well, I guess so."

"Chance Tabor, age thirty-one as of a month ago, founder of Tabor Computer Corporation. Six foot one or two, I'm not sure, about two hundred pounds, I think.''

"You don't know how tall you are?"

"Trivia, my dear. I only store the good stuff like the fact that I like sports, Western music, chocolate chip ice cream and making love to pretty women.''

"Oh, dear me," Brooke whispered.

"I work very hard, enjoy what I do and make big bucks. I have also been searching my entire life for a woman who has nine freckles across the bridge of her nose. You.''

"What?"

"Here's the restaurant. Man, I am starved.''

Yes, food, Brooke thought. She needed some nourishment to rejuvenate herself. Chance Tabor was exhausting! He just . . . zoomed! She didn't fuss with her hair. Did she? And she had nine freckles on her nose? Good grief.

The restaurant was small and cozy with a crackling fire in a hearth against the far wall. Chance helped Brooke off with her coat and draped it on the back of her chair before shrugging out of his jacket.

And there it was. The sweater. It was a black V neck over a steel-gray open-necked shirt, and it molded to Chance's torso exactly the way Brooke had imagined it. He was beautiful.

They ordered from menus printed in both English and Italian, and then Chance leaned back in his chair and crossed his arms over his chest as he stared at Brooke.

"Is something wrong?" she asked.

"Not at all. You're really lovely. In the glow from that candle, your eyes are like brown velvet. I hope that didn't sound corny because I meant it. You're a very attractive woman, Brooke."

"That's quite a line, Mr. Tabor," Brooke said coolly. "Does it usually get results?"

Chance frowned and leaned forward, covering one of her hands with his on the tabletop.

"You don't trust me at all, do you?" he said. "Brooke, I don't play games. I really don't. I deal with facts in my work, and it carries over to my social life. I don't feed improper info into my computers, or deliver phony lines to women. So, you see, Brooke, if I say I find you attractive and nice to be with, I mean it. That's about as honest as I can get."

Honest.

The words seemed to roar in Brooke's ears as she gazed into the blue depths of Chance's eyes. Truth? Spoken from a man with the looks, build and charm of Chance Tabor? He was in the big leagues, the fast lane, the world where Brooke had traveled once and been crushed by deception. Chance had the right to conduct himself however he saw fit, and it was up to her to separate the fabrications and smooth lines from the sincerely spoken words. That was *her* responsibility, and she didn't know how!

In the glow of the candlelight, Chance was looking at her steadily, a soft, gentle expression on his face as though he were waiting for her to say that she accepted what he had said. She couldn't! She didn't want to hear that he had chosen to be with her because she was nice and very attractive. What was next? He desired her more than any other woman before so he needed, wanted, to make love to her? No! She had fallen prey to such passionate pleadings before and never would again.

"Brooke?" Chance said quietly.

"Spaghetti," the waitress said. "Who had the mushroom sauce?"

Chance released Brooke's hand and moved back so that the meal could be placed in front of them. He filled their glasses with wine, and they ate in silence for several minutes.

"Who was he?" Chance finally asked quietly.

"Pardon me?"

"The man who made you so wary, so untrusting. Do you think it's fair to blame all men for something one did?"

"I don't! Chance, you don't understand."

"Try me."

"I am not a bitter woman with some kind of grudge against the male species. There are no rules people are supposed to follow about what they say and do in regard to another person in a relationship. Everyone can be themselves, and each individual has to decide what they want."

"Go on."

"I have to take care of myself. It's up to me. In order to do that, I have to be able to decipher the truth in what I hear."

"And?"

"And I don't do that very well. The men I go out with are all friends. We talk, laugh, have fun. If that changes into hints of promises, declarations of deeper feelings, I know I'm in over my head and I get out. It's not their fault, it's mine. I'm really not bitter, I'm wiser. I'm too trusting, too believing, and so I close my ears to it all so I won't make a mistake again. I have to for my own well-being."

"I see," he said, nodding slightly. "But what happens when you're face-to-face with the real goods and you let it slip through your fingers because you wouldn't believe a word that was said?"

"That's my problem."

"No, damn it, it's not," he said fiercely. "It's mine! I have no intention of lying to you about anything, but I might as well be talking to the wall."

"I—"

"Okay, okay, I get the picture. You blame yourself for not having some kind of sixth sense to know when you're being hustled, conned, and, therefore, you throw out the baby with the bathtub, or however that goes. It makes sense, I guess. Sort of. Man, this is going to be a rough road to go."

"What is?"

"Us. You and me. I wish you'd tell me the name of the guy who did this to you so I could break his face. Maybe I'd feel better. Oh, well, onward and upward. I'll just have to teach you to trust me, that's all. I'll compute this data and evaluate it."

"You're babbling," Brooke said, frowning, "and I'm not understanding a word you're saying."

"Oh? Well, here it is. You're not dusting me off because I told you on our first date that you're pretty and special and I'm glad you're with me. No way. We've just begun, Brooke, and you're going to learn to believe in yourself again so you'll be able to believe in me."

"I don't . . ."

"Hey, don't upset Santa Claus," he said with a smile. "I might do something rash like put coal in stockings. Your spaghetti is getting cold. Eat up."

Brooke started to eat her spaghetti without even tasting it. How had all this happened? She had never, *never*, had a conversation like this with a man. Julie and Gran were the only people that Brooke had ever shared with, told of what she considered to be her major flaw. But there she sat pouring out her innermost feelings to Chance Tabor. What did he plan to do? Feed the juicy information into one of his computers and come up with a printout on how to get her into his bed? Did he see her as some kind of freaky challenge that would be fun to take on and win?

"Now you're angry at yourself for having told me your secret," Chance said.

"It wasn't too bright of me." Brooke frowned.

"Why? Because you're afraid I'll find the whole thing fascinating and I'll decide to break through those barriers just for something to do?"

"The thought did occur to me."

"Brooke, you said we all have the right to conduct ourselves any way we see fit in a relationship, and I suppose that's true. I have never lied to any woman or made promises I didn't intend to keep. I've never intentionally hurt anyone and I never will. We're going to take this slow and easy."

"Why? Why me, Chance?"

"Because," he said, smiling, "not one of the flashy gals I know would sit on a Santa Claus's lap because the Dallas Cowboys lost a football game. You are... enchanting and real and incredibly honest. And, of course, because you have nine freckles on your nose."

"Oh, my," Brooke said with a laugh, "my nose. Are you sure there are nine freckles?"

"Excellent query. Go to the ladies' room and count them. It will be a definite point on my scoreboard that I always tell the truth. Go on."

"You're crazy."

"Go."

"All right." She smiled. "I will!"

Brooke marched off to the ladies' room and returned a few minutes later.

"Nine," she said, sliding back onto her chair.

"See? Truth, justice and the American way."

Their mingled laughter danced through the air, and they consumed the remainder of their dinner with friendly banter on various topics, including the merits of the pro football teams. Chance was a true-blue Packers fan, and Brooke moaned in disgust. He informed her that her Cowboys were not exactly at the top of the league, and on it went. It was fun. Brooke pushed from her mind the earlier conversation when she had bared her soul to Chance and simply enjoyed herself. He was charming and witty and, without a doubt, the most handsome man in the restaurant.

"How did you get a tan in the dead of winter?" she asked as they drank their coffee. "Do you ski?"

"Yep. I was in Aspen for the first snow. It was great. Do *you* ski?"

"Not very well, but I enjoy the atmosphere at the lodges and the snow. I watch the people and pretend I just came in from the toughest slopes. Julie is a terrific skier. With those long legs of hers, she just flies. I'm her cheering section."

"You two are very close, aren't you?"

"Yes, we've shared the apartment for three years, and we met in business school."

"That's really nice. Good friends are hard to come by. I have a couple of buddies that mean a great deal to me. They're both married now and have families so I don't hang out with them as much as I did."

"You've never been married?"

"No, but I intend to be. I want to be a father, too. Did you ever spend time in England?"

"No why?"

"You put your fork on your plate sideways like the British do."

"One of the housekeepers my father hired to care for me was English. You don't miss anything, do you?"

"Not if I can help it." He smiled. "Where is your father?"

"In France at the moment. He's a correspondent. My mother died when I was very young, and I was raised by different women. They were all marvelous and adored me. I had a nice childhood really."

"You don't feel cheated because you didn't have a normal family?"

"No, why should I?"

"You're quite a lady, Brooke Bradley," Chance said quietly. "The more I hear, the more I like. Oops, I made you nervous. You're playing with those curls again."

"Oh, for Pete's sake." She laughed, dropping her hand from her hair. "You'll know I'm shook up when you see me diving into a hot fudge sundae."

"Ah, data," he said, tapping his temple. "I'll store that away."

They were smiling when they emerged into the frosty night and were greeted by large, damp snowflakes falling from the sky.

"Beautiful," Chance said as they walked to the car. "But wet. My hair is going to get curly. I hate it."

"Oh, how sweet." Brooke smiled.

"Grim. Get in the car."

Chance drove carefully on the slick streets but with a relaxed attitude that indicated he was accustomed to handling a vehicle in the snowy weather. He bellowed in dismay when a curl flipped onto his forehead, and Brooke laughed in delight.

"Do you realize what this hair does for my macho image?" he asked. "It's disgusting. A male Shirley Temple. I should move to Arizona where it's hot and dry. Or Texas. I wonder how I'd look decked out like a cowboy."

Fantastic, that's how, Brooke thought. Chance would be gorgeous in any type of clothing or . . . in none at all. Heav-

ens, where had that come from? That tall, strong, beautifully proportioned body glistening in the glow from a
fireplace or...

Brooke shifted in her seat as tingling fingers of desire
danced across her senses, and she felt a flush creep onto her
cheeks. She was not behaving like herself. For the first year
after Chuck's betrayal, she had been a virtual recluse, re-
pairing her broken heart and shattered self-esteem. She had
emerged at last from her cocoon of confusion with an inner
acceptance of her inability to trust her own judgment about
men. Tentatively beginning to date again, she had chosen
the safe escorts, the ones who wanted nothing more than a
carefree evening and a good-night kiss. Those who stepped
over her invisible line were sent packing.

But Chance was different. He was upsetting her well-
ordered life. She had told him her secrets, was continually
held immobile under the visual embraces from his blue, blue
eyes, and now? Now, for Pete's sake, she was picturing the
man undressed! It was absurd. She had to get a grip on herself!

"Do you eat breakfast?" Chance asked.

"Yes."

"Great. How about going out for breakfast tomorrow
morning? The most efficient way to do this would be for me
to spend the night with you, but since that isn't going to
happen, I'll pick you up at nine, okay? A big breakfast is the
perfect way to start the weekend."

"All right," Brooke said, smiling. "It's a date."

In the elevator in her building, Brooke fiddled with the
curls on her right cheek and frowned. Chance was going to
kiss her, she knew it, and she was a bundle of nerves. If she
got shaky when he looked at her, what would happen when
he pulled her into his arms?

"I'm not going to bite you," he said quietly. "You really
are quite safe with me."

"I know that," she said, a little too sharply.

"No, you don't. That's the problem. But we're doing fine so don't worry about a thing. Do you have your key?"

Chance unlocked the door, pushed it open and stepped back for Brooke to enter. She took off her coat and only then realized that he was still standing out in the hall.

"Aren't you coming in?" she asked.

"I wasn't invited."

"Do come in, Mr. Tabor," she said with a smile. "Would you like some coffee?"

"Sure," he said, shrugging out of his jacket. "Is Julie sleeping? Should I whisper?"

"No, she isn't home. She and Joey were going to a concert."

"Joey? Someone special?"

"Joey Rather."

"The pro basketball player? He retired, right?"

"Yes, he hurt his knee and never was up to par again. He owns half of a radio station here. He and Julie have been seeing each other for about six months. I swear, Joey is the tallest man I have ever met. He's really nice, too, and they make a gorgeous couple. They're both so slim and tall."

"I'll be looking forward to meeting them."

"Sit down while I make some coffee."

Brooke busied herself in the kitchen and was aware of the exact moment when Chance stood in the doorway. She didn't see him, she just knew he was there, and her hand trembled slightly as she placed a cup on the tray. Chance moved slowly forward and stopped close to her, leaning against the counter.

"Brooke," he said, his voice a low, husky whisper.

That was all Chance said, just her name, but Brooke felt as though she had been stroked by dark velvet. Her skin tingled and her heart raced as she slowly lifted her lashes to gaze into the fathomless depths of Chance's blue eyes.

Chance slowly straightened his stance and then lifted his large hands to cup her face. His warm breath fluttered over her lips and then he kissed her. He kissed her so softly, so gently that unexpected tears sprung to Brooke's eyes. He lifted his head and gazed for a long moment into her glistening eyes and then, as though she were made of fragile china, gathered her close to his chest and claimed her mouth again. His tongue sought entry, and she complied as she leaned further into his rugged length.

A soft purr escaped from Brooke's throat as wondrous sensations swept through her. The feel, the taste, the aroma of Chance Tabor made her light-headed, causing her to splay her hands tightly on his back for support. It was a kiss like none she had ever experienced before, and she didn't wish it to end. She was floating away to an unknown place, and she wanted to go.

There was nothing intimidating about the strength in the arms that held her, for they seemed to represent a safe haven, a sense of coming home. Brooke felt the desire stir within her and welcomed it as she might a forgotten friend who had at last returned. The kiss drugged her senses; it was heavenly.

"You see?" Chance said, lifting his head and taking a ragged breath. "Nothing to worry about at all. Nothing except the fact that I would like to go on kissing you for the next hour straight. I think . . . you'd better pour the coffee."

"Yes. Certainly," Brooke said, positive that he could hear the wild beating of her heart. "But you'll have to let me go."

"Am I still holding you?" He smiled. "Son of a gun, I am. But you feel like an angel in my arms, Brooke Bradley. And, oh, you do kiss like a dream."

"Chance, I . . ."

"Coffee," he said, releasing her at last. "Any cookies in that container marked Flour?"

"Yes, but how did you know?"

"You took coffee out of the one marked sugar. That says you're not into baking so you store cookies in the flour bin. Correct?"

"Correct. I do have some sugar cubes if you want them for your coffee. Have you ever considered being an international spy or a detective?"

"Nope. They get shot at. Besides, I like my computers."

"Just what exactly do you do?" Brooke asked, relieved that her breathing had returned to normal.

"I'll carry the tray," he said, picking it up and following her from the room. "Well, we go in and analyze a company's needs, then write a program for their specific operation. It's very challenging."

"You say we. Do you have people working for you?"

"There are three others. Two men, a woman and, of course, a secretary we all drive crazy."

"That's quite an operation for someone so young," Brooke said, sitting down next to him on the sofa.

"It's been hard work but worth it. I'm bidding on out-of-state jobs now, expanding my operation."

"Doesn't that mean a great deal of traveling?" Brooke asked, aware that she was registering a vague sense of disappointment.

"Some. I divide it up so no one is away too much. The actual programming is done here, though. We go in, analyze the business, see what kind of equipment they need, such as the size of the computer capacity, dot-matrix or daisy wheel printer, that type of thing, and come back and write their program."

"Daisy wheel?"

"Oh, that's a printer that produces letter-perfect printouts for correspondence when you're using word processing. It depends on the type of business whether they need... Am I confusing you?"

"No more than if you were speaking a foreign language." Brooke laughed. "I work for an attorney and have a plain old electric typewriter. The silly thing can't even spell."

"I guess I got a little carried away." Chance frowned. "We'll talk about something else."

"When you say size of computer do you mean how much room it takes up in the office?"

Chance looked at her with a startled expression that changed into a warm, gentle smile. He didn't speak, he simply gazed at her, his blue eyes locking onto her mahogany ones.

"Dumb question?" Brooke said weakly.

"Lovely question," he said quietly, leaning slowly toward her. "It means random access memory, not physical size. It's measured in Ks, like 64K...or 128K... or..."

The kiss was urgent, almost frenzied, as their tongues met in the sweet darkness of Brooke's mouth. She lifted her arms to circle Chance's neck, sinking her hands into the thick, dark waves of his hair, winding her fingers through the errant curls. Chance pulled her close, his large hands flattening on her back to press her breasts to the rock-hard wall of his chest.

Chance lifted his head a fraction to draw a steadying breath and then took possession of her mouth once more as he shifted slightly to lean her back against the throw pillows. His hands slid to the sides of her breasts, filling his palms with their fullness. His thumbs trailed over her nipples, which grew taut even beneath the heavy material of her sweater.

Brooke was awash with desire. Chance felt so good and smelled so good, and she seemed to be falling into a rosy sphere of oblivion. But from somewhere in the back of her mind a voice sounded, calling to her to come back to reality, to comprehend what she was doing, to question what was taking place.

"Chance," she gasped. "No!"

He lifted his head and looked at her, his blue eyes almost smoky gray and radiating a readable message of desire. With a shuddering breath he sat up, shaking his head slightly as if to come out of a trance, then leaned his elbows on his knees and ran his hand down his face.

Brooke struggled to sit up, then fluffed her hair in a nervous gesture as she looked at Chance anxiously.

"I'm sorry," she said softly.

"Damn it, don't say that!" he roared, causing her to jump. "Do not apologize for something I did. Understand?"

"Well, you don't have to get so crabby!"

"Oh, Brooke—" he chuckled, his features softening as he pulled her close "—you are terrific. You really are. I'm going home now. Remember that we have a date for breakfast, okay?"

"Okay."

"Tonight was wonderful. Thank you," he said, kissing her on the forehead. "I'll let myself out. Put your nine freckles to bed and dream about me."

"Good night, Chance," Brooke said softly.

Long after Chance had gone, Brooke sat on the sofa and stared at nothing in particular. She recounted each moment of the evening, trying to determine why she had told Chance Tabor of the flaw in her personality, the lack of insight into men's motives. And why she had responded with such abandonment to his kisses. And why she had dreaded the thought of him being out of town a great deal. And why, and why, and why, to so many confusing questions that hammered in her mind. But there were no answers.

There was only one thing that Brooke was certain of.

Chance Tabor was scary as hell.

That was the bottom line and the thought that Brooke took into her sleep, which resulted in a restless slumber and disturbing dreams. Chance appeared in her subconscious as Santa Claus, then as a cowboy riding a Saint Bernard as big as a horse. He was there smiling that beautiful smile, and then he opened a door on an enormous computer and disappeared inside, out of her view and out of her reach.

Brooke awoke the next morning with a headache and stumbled into the bathroom for two aspirin. She peered into Julie's room and saw her roommate burrowed deep under the covers. Pulling the door closed, Brooke set coffee on to drip, then showered and dressed in red wool slacks and a red-and-white sweater. What she did not do was think. She had a sneaking suspicion that, if she dwelled on the subject of Chance Tabor, she would hide in the closet and refuse to answer the door when he came. So she blanked her mind and smiled when she opened the door to him at precisely nine o'clock.

"Hi, Brooke," he said, stepping into the room. "Do I whisper this time? Is Julie asleep?"

"She sleeps like a dead person," Brooke said. "We won't wake her."

"Ready for pancakes? Waffles? Bacon and eggs? All of the above?"

"Well, one of them."

"Ready for a good-morning kiss?" he said, pulling her into his arms.

Oh, yes, she was definitely ready for one of *those*, Brooke thought, as Chance covered her mouth with his.

"Mmm," he said when he released her. "You taste better than maple syrup."

"Thank you, I think." She laughed.

A winter sun was rapidly melting the snow and they could only see patches in the shadows and under trees. Chance drove to a quaint restaurant across town that was decorated like a Swiss chalet.

"Eat plenty," he said as they glanced at their menus. "We'll need a lot of energy for our project."

"What project?"

"Our snowman—the one we're going to build."

"We are?" Brooke asked. "Why?"

"Because there is a park a block from here that doesn't even have a snowman and because it will be fun and because that way I won't have to take you home after we eat. Get it?"

"Got it."

"Good."

The snowman was, Chance declared loudly, a masterpiece. It was taller than Brooke and slightly lopsided, had sticks for arms and flat stones for its eyes and nose. It had taken a great deal of effort to build since they'd had to collect the snow from beneath the trees. The snowman was also melting.

"Don't you dare!" Chance hollered to the sun. "Don't you appreciate art?"

"Ohhh, I'm frozen," Brooke moaned. "I can't feel my feet, and I think my nose fell off."

"Nope, it's there, complete with nine freckles," Chance said, giving the subject matter a noisy kiss. "Come with me, my dear, and I shall warm you up."

"Oh?"

"Hot cider. Sound superb?"

"Indeed."

"Oh, cripes! The snowman's head slipped off! Let's get out of here. This is breaking my heart."

Brooke smiled and allowed herself to be pulled close to Chance's side as they walked to the car. It had been a crazy, carefree and fun morning, and she felt lighthearted and happy. Whatever distressing thoughts that might have lingered from the dark hours of the night were forgotten and replaced by euphoric bliss.

Chance drove through the busy Saturday traffic and pulled into an underground garage.

"I have to take you to my apartment because that's where the cider is," he said, turning off the ignition and grinning at Brooke.

"At least cider is more original than etchings."

"You can't be too shook up. You haven't tugged on your curls yet."

"Only because my fingers are frozen." Brooke smiled as she got out of the car.

"My abode," Chance said a short time later after they had ridden the elevator up to the tenth floor and walked down a carpeted hallway. "Come in and get toasty."

The living room was large and decorated in pale grays and pastel blues. Brooke wandered forward slowly and glanced around the expanse. Everything was obviously of the finest quality and very expensive, but it lacked warmth, a homey feeling.

"It's nice," she said.

"No, it's not," Chance said with a laugh. "It's awful. I turned a decorator loose in here, and this is what I got. Grim. It's called early hospital, I believe. Cold, sterile, blah."

"It wouldn't take much to fix it up. All it needs is some color."

"Want the job? I'll hire you."

"Nope."

"Damn. Well, take off your coat and your shoes and socks, and I'll get us some cider."

Brooke did as she was instructed and then curled up in the corner of the comfortable but drab sofa.

"Here you go," Chance said, handing her a mug and sitting down. "Complete with cinnamon stick. Now, let's fix those footsies."

Before Brooke could protest, Chance swung her legs around and rested her feet on his muscular thighs where he began to gently massage them. He wore a royal-blue sweater and tight, faded jeans, and his hair was an ebony glow of thick waves on his head. Brooke felt her breath catch in her throat as the heat from Chance's hands seemed to travel throughout her entire body.

"Getting warmer?" he asked.

"Yes," she said, hoping to the heavens that her voice hadn't squeaked.

"If you had a Saint Bernard, he could sit on your feet, but I think this is much nicer. You have cute toes complete with pretty pink polish. You're so feminine, Brooke. Everything about you is so delicate, lovely. You make a man very aware of his own strength and the marvelous differences in the way our bodies are put together. Oh, yes, Brooke Bradley, I am very glad I'm a man because that means there's hope that you'll become my lady. My lady. That's a way of saying I want to make love to you, make you mine."

"Chance!"

"Feet warm enough?"

"Yes, fine, thank you," she said, pulling them off his lap.

"We're based on honesty, remember? So I'm being honest. I do want you, Brooke. I'm not going to force the issue or get bent out of shape when you refuse to go to bed with me, though. I understand that you don't totally trust me yet, and I can handle that. But when we do make love, it's going to be an incredibly beautiful experience."

"It is?" Brooke said, hardly able to breathe.

"Yes," he said, taking the mug from her hand and placing it on the coffee table as he moved close to her, "it is."

Chance kissed her cheeks, her forehead, each eyelid, the end of her nose, before brushing his lips across hers. The foray over her face had been as light as a butterfly's wings, yet it had left Brooke trembling. When he claimed her mouth at last in a fierce embrace, she thought she would shout for joy. Her tongue moved to meet his, and waves of desire rambled through her.

Chance's hands slid under the waistband of her sweater and rested on the smooth skin of her back, which was instantly warmed by his touch. His breathing became labored as the kiss intensified, his tongue delving deep into Brooke's mouth in a rhythmic motion that brought a roaring noise to her ears.

"Brooke," Chance murmured close to her lips, "will you come into the bedroom with me?"

Three

—

What!'' Brooke shrieked, pushing against Chance's chest with such force that he toppled backward against the pillows.

Chance's shocked expression changed almost at once, and he whooped with laughter, the deep, rumbly sound seeming to echo through the room. He attempted to speak, only to start laughing again, gasping for air.

Brooke jumped to her feet and planted her hands on her hips.

"You're despicable!" she yelled.

"No, wait!" Chance said, struggling to sit up.

"I'm leaving!" Brooke said, reaching for her soggy socks.

"Brooke, I didn't mean—" Chance said, scrambling to his feet. "I asked you to come into the bedroom—"

"I heard you! Oh, these socks are cold!"

"To talk to me while I pack! I have to catch a plane for San Diego."

"What?" she said, spinning around to face him, the socks hanging limply from her hands.

"That's why I wanted to see you this morning. I have to go out of town on a job for a few days. I had such a great time last night. I hated to go away without seeing you first."

"Oh," she said softly.

"Okay?" he said, taking the socks and dropping them on the floor. Moving closer, he brushed his lips across hers. "You don't mind that I wanted to be with you, do you?"

"No," she murmured, her heart pounding.

"Because I like being with you very much," he said, trailing a ribbon of kisses down her neck. "So if you'll come watch me pack, I won't have to take you home quite so soon."

"That . . . sounds very nice," she said, her breath catching in her throat.

"I wish I wasn't leaving," he said, close to her lips.

"Me . . . too."

"Come with me?"

"To San Diego?" she said, stiffening in his arms.

"No, the bedroom!" he said, taking her by the hand.

The bedroom was decorated with as much lifeless flair as the living room, and Brooke sat in a pale blue velvet chair while Chance pulled a suitcase out of the closet and set it on the bed, which was covered with an ivory spread.

"Why do you have to go on a weekend?" she asked.

"I'll meet with the owner of the company tomorrow, and we'll be able to go over his records without interruption. It's more efficient. Are your feet cold? You can wear a pair of my socks."

"No, they're fine."

"Shall I bring you a surprise from the Coast? An orange? Sand? A seashell? A Saint Bernard?"

"No," Brooke said with a laugh. "I'll pass on all of those, thanks."

"Then I'll bring you home...me. How's that? Not good, huh? You're frowning."

"You just move so quickly, Chance. It's hard to keep up with you. After all, we hardly know each other."

"Oh, I think we do," he said, rummaging in the dresser drawer. "Where are my clean handkerchiefs? Oh, yeah, they're in the kitchen."

"Really? Why?"

"In case I sneeze while I'm cooking. Paper towels are very rough on the nose. Don't you think we've discovered a great deal about each other since we met?"

"Oh, Chance," Brooke said, laughing, "having a conversation with you is like talking to a cyclone."

"Really?" He frowned. "I understand everything I say. There, I'm all packed. Oops, forgot my shaving stuff."

As Chance went into the bathroom, Brooke shook her head and smiled. Chance was incredible, she thought. There were so many facets to him that he could appeal to every type of the female species. The sexy, sultry numbers would go straight after that body, the intellectuals were dealing with a near genius and the ones who would mother him had his boyish ways and somewhat absentminded nature. Oh, yes, Chance Tabor had it all, and Brooke found him to be absolutely enchanting.

"All set?" Chance asked, returning to the bedroom and snapping the suitcase closed.

"Yes," she said, getting to her feet.

"Here, wear these socks. You'll catch cold for sure if you put yours on."

Chance handed her a pair of white sports socks with red and blue stripes at the top, and she sat down on the edge of the bed to pull them on.

"Brooke Bradley on my bed!" he yelled. "I've waited a lifetime for this!"

"You're a cuckoo," she said, laughing.

"I figure you're my Christmas present. I have an in with Santa Claus," he said, sitting down next to her and circling her shoulders with his arm.

"Yes, but are you naughty or nice?"

"Wrong question," he said, lowering his lips to hers. "Ask me if I'm any good."

As Chance claimed her mouth, Brooke had the irrational thought that she was falling, only to realize that Chance was gently lowering her back onto the bed. Her toes lifted off the floor as he slid one arm around her waist and kept the other across her shoulders. His tongue delved deep into her mouth, then pulled back to duel seductively with hers.

Heat coursed through Brooke's body as she lifted her hands to sink her fingers into the ebony depths of Chance's hair. His hand slid under the waistband of her sweater and blazed a trail upward, coming to rest at her breast pushing above the lacy material of her bra. The rosy bud grew taut under the stroking rhythm of Chance's thumb, and she arched her back toward him to bring the tantalizing sensations closer.

As Brooke moved her hands to Chance's back, she could feel his steely muscles trembling beneath his sweater, and as he shifted slightly, she felt the evidence of his arousal pressing against her.

She wasn't being fair and she knew it, but, oh, he made her desires soar and her femininity rejoice in its existence. Where he was rugged, she was soft, and the contrast was ecstasy itself. His lips and tongue wove a spell of sweet magic over her sense of reasoning, and his hands were instruments of pleasure. But she had to stop this before it went too far.

"Chance, I . . ."

"It's okay," he said, his voice strained. "I just want to kiss you, touch you. I'll have such sweet memories to take to California with me. You feel so good, Brooke. So good."

With maddening slowness Chance withdrew his hand from beneath Brooke's sweater and, after one last searing kiss, turned and sat up on the edge of the bed. He drew a steadying breath and then with a gentle smile reached for Brooke and pulled her up next to him, kissing her on the temple. He laced his fingers through hers and neither spoke. They simply sat there, and a strange shroud of contentment washed over Brooke.

Chance had asked nothing more of her than he knew she was willing to give, and Brooke felt warm and cherished and, oh, so special. Kissing, touching her created memories for Chance? Lovely thoughts that he could tuck away in his mind and take on his trip? How could that be? A virile man like Chance Tabor would remember the feel of her lips and her soft skin and not become angry that it had ended before they made love? Chance, who probably needed a cold shower, had smiled at her with infinite gentleness and understanding?

"Why?" Brooke said, not realizing that she had spoken out loud.

"Hmmm?"

"Chance, why are you being so patient with me?"

"Because you're worth it. Put those socks on and off we go."

Brooke managed to get her feet into her wet shoes despite the enormous socks, and they were soon driving back to her apartment.

"Man, I'm running late," Chance said, glancing at his watch.

"Then just drop me off and don't take the time to park."

"I hate to do that."

"You can't miss your plane, Chance."

"Yeah, okay."

There were no free parking spaces in front of Brooke's building so Chance simply stopped in the flow of traffic, hauled Brooke into his arms and kissed her deeply.

"You can't do this," she said breathlessly.

"But I adore kissing you."

"I mean hold up traffic."

"Oh, well, it's the Christmas season. Everyone is very tolerant and forgiving. Goodbye, Brooke," he said, kissing her again. "I'll see you soon."

"Bye, Chance. Thank you for a lovely morning."

Brooke hurried to the sidewalk and waved as Chance smiled broadly at her. He gave a thumbs-up sign to the drivers behind him and in a few minutes had disappeared from view. Brooke registered a disconcerting sense of emptiness, as if the sunshine had gone out of her day, and then walked slowly into the building.

Julie was folding clean laundry when Brooke entered the apartment.

"Hi, Beebee," Julie said. "Where did you disappear to?"

"The North Pole."

"With Santa Claus?"

"Yep."

"Really? What did you do?"

"We had dinner last night and breakfast this morning."

"What happened between dinner and breakfast?"

"I was in bed. Here. Alone."

"Rats."

"Julie!"

"Seriously, Beebee, what kind of person is Chance? Did you enjoy his company? And most of all, what does he look like?"

"He is...beautiful. His hair is dark and wavy and curls when it gets wet, and he has shoulders eight miles wide, and he's nice."

"You're blushing."

"I am not!"

"You have a glowy look about you."

"Oh, stop. I spent some time in the company of a handsome man. Big deal. I've got to get out of these shoes," Brooke said, pulling them off.

"I love it! Julie laughed. "Is Chance the computer corporation?"

"Yes, and he sort of thinks like a computer. I mean, well, he's very observant and then he analyzes what he's seen and heard and draws a conclusion."

"Superbrain, huh?"

"Very. Oh, Julie, I don't know, he's so many people rolled up into one gorgeous hunk of stuff. I'm sure he's used to very worldly women—"

"Who sleep around."

"Exactly. But yet he claims he likes being with me and wants to see me again even though—"

"You don't sleep around."

"Right. Now I ask you. Does that make sense?"

"You're selling yourself short again, Beebee. You have a lot to offer a man."

"Providing he's the right one, and you and I both know how good I am at determining that. If I was really smart, I wouldn't see Chance again, but I have a feeling my brain short-circuited the minute he looked at me with those incredible blue eyes. Which, by the way, are naturally that color and not tinted contacts."

"I'm glad we didn't have a bet on that one. Are you going out with Chance tonight?"

"No, he just left for the airport to catch a plane for San Diego for a business trip. That's why we had breakfast instead."

"After just spending last evening together?"

"Well, yes."

"Interesting," Julie said thoughtfully.

"Don't get crazy, Julie," Brooke said, heading for the kitchen. "Two dates does not a love affair make. How's Joey?"

"His usual sexy self," Julie called. "We're going Christmas shopping later. Want to come?"

"No, thanks. You two just go and enjoy."

An hour later Joey arrived, and he and Julie headed out to join the throngs who were busily preparing for the holiday ahead. Brooke wandered around the empty apartment, suddenly restless. She flopped onto the sofa and propped her feet on top, wiggling her toes in Chance's socks.

Chance. An image of his face formed in her mind, and she could almost hear his rich, throaty laughter. Even his special male aroma seemed to reach her senses, as did the remembrance of his touch and kiss. Desire tingled through her body, and she allowed it entry, savoring it. Had she been so easily aroused by Chuck Finley? She could hardly remember what he looked like, let alone what tempestuous emotions that he may have evoked in her. But somehow she felt new, different, when she was with Chance, as if she were standing on the edge of an unexplored frontier.

Would she venture forth? Take Chance's hand and be led to where she had not gone before? No, she couldn't, wouldn't succumb to his vibrant masculinity and gently spoken words. To do so was to place her emotional well-being in his care, and she wasn't prepared to do that. It would call for trust, for the serene knowledge that all she saw and heard was honest and real, and that was beyond her scope. To believe in Chance was to believe in her own ability to judge what was true and that... was her flaw.

The apartment seemed suddenly too empty, too lonely, and Brooke went across the hall to visit Gran, only to find that the older woman was not at home. Everyone, apparently, was filled with Christmas spirit and out shopping for the perfect gifts for friends and family. Brooke had little to purchase, and the treasures were safely tucked away on her closet shelf.

The afternoon passed slowly, and Brooke found herself becoming increasingly depressed. She was unable to pinpoint the cause of her gloomy mood and finally blanked her thoughts by watching an old movie on television. When Julie and Joey had not returned by dinnertime, Brooke assumed they had gone out to eat. Brooke consumed a can of soup, a half box of crackers and a bowl of ice cream. When the telephone rang, she walked to it slowly and answered with a rather listless greeting.

"Ho ho ho," a deep voice said.

"Chance!" Brooke said, an instant smile on her face.

"Hi, Brooke. Good thing our snowman isn't out here. He wouldn't have lasted five minutes because it's really hot. Why are you so bummed out? Hey, is it because you miss me? Great! I miss you, too. Hop a plane and we'll go to dinner. Seriously, why are you down? Your hello was less than sparkling."

"I'm fine. Really."

"You're not catching cold from getting your feet wet, are you?"

"No. Your socks kept me toasty warm. In fact, I still have them on."

"Hey, that's nice. I like that. I guess that sounds silly, but I'm a sentimental guy. You should see this hotel room. It's decorated better than my apartment, which doesn't say a helluva lot for my apartment."

They chatted for several more minutes, and Brooke was smiling the whole time. Chance finally said that he had to go because a shopping trip was on his agenda. He'd forgotten to pack his shirts.

"I'll see you soon," he said. "Think about me."

"I will. Goodbye, Chance."

"Brooke?"

"Yes?"

"Smile, okay? 'Tis the season to be jolly."

"I'm smiling, Chance," she said softly. "Bye."

Brooke slowly replaced the receiver and then wrapped her arms around her elbows in a protective gesture. Her earlier depression had been whisked away by the mere sound of Chance's voice. A part of her mind was singing a happy tune, was euphoric because Chance had thought of her and had called her from San Diego. But a small, niggling voice made her face the fact that her mood switch was entirely due to Chance Tabor. And, even worse, her gloom-and-doom state had been because she had wanted to see him, touch him, be the recipient of one of his sensuous kisses.

"This will never do!" she said aloud. "I hardly know that man. He can't possibly be having this great an impact on my life. Can he?"

In a frustrated gesture Brooke threw up her hands and went to Gran's. The older woman had indeed been Christmas shopping and complained loudly that her feet hurt. The two engaged in a tournament of gin rummy, betting with colored marshmallows. Brooke pushed Chance Tabor from her mind and concentrated on her cards. Because she ate all the marshmallows that she won, she was not feeling well when she reentered the apartment at nine.

"That you, Beebee?" Julie called from the kitchen.

"Yes."

"Want some hot chocolate?"

"Ugh. No, thanks. I just OD'd on marshmallows."

"Hi, Beebee," Joey said, coming out of the kitchen. "How's things with you and Santa?"

"Strange," Brooke said, flopping onto the sofa. "He's a very unsettling man."

"He's into computers, huh?"

"Yes. He owns a company and is obviously very good at what he does. I've never met anyone like him, Joey."

"Is that bad?"

"No, but I think he's out of my league. In fact, I know he is."

"Ridiculous," Julie said, coming into the room carrying a tray. "He's handsome and rich and sexy. So what?"

"Yeah," Joey said, laughing, "I'm all of those things and I'm terrific."

"Oh, brother," Julie said. "Have some hot chocolate."

"Seriously, Beebee," Joey said, "I've never seen you so uptight about a guy. What's his name?"

"Chance Tabor."

"Why don't you just go with it for now and see what happens?" Joey said. "You'll never know unless you—"

"Give Chance a chance!" Julie yelled.

"I'll think about it," Brooke said. "Let's talk about something else."

The three watched a Christmas special on television, and then Brooke said good night and went to bed. Her dreams were again haunted by images of Chance, and she woke before dawn to stare into the darkness.

When Brooke shuffled into the kitchen later for a cup of coffee, the gasped as she found Julie sitting at the table crying.

"Julie, what's wrong?" Brooke said, sitting down opposite her.

"Oh, Beebee, last night after you went to bed, Joey asked me to marry him."

"That's wonderful! Oh, Julie, I'm so happy for you! No, wait. Brides-to-be don't cry."

"I love Joey, I really do. He's everything I've ever dreamed about in a man, but . . ."

"But what?" Brooke asked gently.

"Beebee, for as long as I can remember, I've wanted to be a model. The few jobs I've been able to get have reaffirmed that in my mind. But Joey wants to buy a home right away so we can start a family. I'm going to have to make a choice. I can't be married, pregnant, all that stuff, and still go after my career. Joey won't settle for a part-time wife. He comes from a broken home, and he has what he wants all figured out. I'm so damned confused."

"What did Joey say when you told him?"

"He was terribly hurt. I said I needed some time to get my head on straight, and he looked so stricken. He wanted to hear that I'd marry him, have a baby as soon as possible, and I just couldn't say yes. I have to think!"

"Joey loves you. I'm sure he'll be patient once he calms down."

"I don't know. He was so quiet when he left, so sad. It would have been better if he'd hollered, but the look on his face was . . . Oh, what am I going to do?"

"Take all the time you need, that's what. You're talking about the rest of your life. You've got to be very sure you're doing what is right for you."

"I love my Joey!" Julie wailed. "But, but, oh, hell!"

"Well said. There's the phone. I bet that's Joey right now."

It was not Joey Rather calling; it was Chance Tabor.

"Did I wake you?" he asked.

"No, I was up," Brooke said.

"Just thought I'd say good morning before I head out of here and earn my keep."

"What? Oh, yes, I hope you have a good day."

"You sound preoccupied."

"I'm sorry, Chance. Julie is upset this morning, and I don't seem to have anything brilliant to say to her that will cheer her up."

"She's got problems, huh? Ten bucks says it has to do with Joey Rather."

"How did you know?"

"Because probably half the tears shed in this world have something to do with affairs of the heart. I hope they fix up whatever is out of kilter."

"Me, too. They're both very special."

"So are you, Brooke Bradley. I can tell how concerned you are about them. I feel like I'm on the outside looking in on a loving group. Well, I'll just have to earn my way in. That's reasonable. But I'll tell you something. You and I are going to be a happening, a wondrous thing. I know you don't trust me a helluva lot, but that's okay. For now. It's a temporary situation."

"Chance, I—"

"Gotta run. Tell Julie to perk up. Things have a way of working themselves out. Smile, ladies. That's an order from Santa Claus. I'll talk to you later. Bye."

"Goodbye, Chance."

"Was that Chance?" Julie said, coming into the living room.

"Yes."

"That is one very attentive man. Would you like to join a convent with me? Life would be so much simpler."

Brooke hugged Julie and then the two ate breakfast and cleaned up the kitchen. Joey arrived unannounced just after ten and appeared exhausted. A subdued Julie left the apartment with him, and Brooke had the irrational thought that they looked as if they were on their way to a funeral.

Love, Brooke decided, was a killer.

When the telephone rang after lunch, Brooke purposely issued a cheerful greeting, just in case it was Chance.

"Beebee?"

"Dad?"

"Hi, sugar."

"This is a surprise, Dad. Where are you?"

"I'm in London now. Honey, I'm afraid I won't be home for Christmas like I promised. I'm going straight to Ireland from here. I'm really sorry, but I'm sure you understand."

"Of course," Brooke said quietly.

"I'll mail your gift, okay? We'll have a nice dinner together when I get back. We don't have to celebrate Christmas on the exact day. After all, it's not as though you believe in Santa Claus anymore."

"No, I . . . I don't," Brooke said, the image of Chance flashing before her eyes. "I mean, I sort of do. No, I certainly do not."

"What did you say, honey?"

"Nothing, Dad. I'll be thinking of you on Christmas. Have a nice holiday."

"Love ya, pumpkin. Bye."

"Wonderful," Brooke said, replacing the receiver. "What else can go wrong? This is a lousy, crummy day!" She mustn't slip and let Julie know about Mac Bradley's change in plans. Julie was going home to California for Christmas and would have a fit if she knew that Brooke was going to be alone. Even Gran was leaving Denver for a special senior citizens' holiday in Aspen. "I'll be fine," Brooke said firmly. "It's okay. No, it's not! It's awful. I hate it!"

On impulse Brooke bundled up and left the apartment to spend the rest of the afternoon wandering through stores and trying to restore her Christmas spirit. She entertained the idea of returning to the mall where she had met Chance with the hope of getting a glimpse of his notorious grandfather playing Santa but dismissed the thought as being silly. Julie had not returned to the apartment by ten that night, Chance did not call and Brooke went to bed with a dejected sigh. The best plan would be to go to sleep, she decided, and not wake up until New Year's Day.

When Brooke entered the kitchen the next morning, she found a note from Julie stating that Julie would call in sick to the office and was not going to work. Brooke peered into Julie's room and saw her roommate flung across the bed fully clothed, sound asleep. What time she had gotten in and what had transpired with Joey, Brooke did not know. She could only wait until she returned home that evening to see if Julie wished to discuss it.

The attorney Brooke worked for was a congenial man in his fifties with grown children and grandchildren that he never tired of talking about. He handled a variety of work, which created ongoing challenges for Brooke. She enjoyed the intricacies of law and produced error-free documents for her employer.

"Good morning, Brooke," her boss said as he entered the office.

"Hello, Mr. Wilson."

"I have a surprise for you."

"Oh?"

"I'm closing the office on Christmas Eve day and two days after Christmas, with pay for you, of course. You'll have an opportunity to really enjoy the holidays."

"Thank you, that's very generous of you," Brooke said, forcing a smile. "The extra time off will be... lovely."

"You deserve it. You work very hard for me. Well, down to business. I need to dictate some letters."

"Certainly," Brooke said. Oh, rats! she thought miserably. Extra hours on her hands to be alone when everyone else was with their loved ones or off having a good time. Her boss had just given her a bonus that was the last thing she needed. Was there no justice?

Brooke was late leaving the office because a last-minute client needed a contract typed, and she inched her way home through the rush-hour traffic. When she entered the living room at the apartment, her eyes widened at the sight before her, and a knot tightened painfully in her stomach.

Julie Mason was being held tightly in Chance Tabor's arms.

"Hi, Brooke," Chance said as he patted Julie on the back. "I'm home from California."

"Yes, I guess you are," Brooke said, blinking once slowly with the fervent hope that Julie would disappear into thin air.

"I'm sorry, Chance," Julie sniffled, stepping out of his embrace. "I didn't mean to fall apart. It's been such a gruesome day. Hi, Beebee."

"Who?" Chance said.

"Me," Brooke said. "It started out as initials. You know, Brooke Bradley, B. B., then my dad started spelling it like a name and... Hold it! I demand to know why my best friend was in the arms of my... my... Ignore me. I'm not making sense."

"Oh, sweet bliss," Chance said to the heavens. "She's jealous! This is my lucky day."

"I am not jealous!" Brooke said.

"Could have fooled me," Chance said, grinning at her. "May I kiss you hello now?"

"No!"

"Beebee," Julie said, "Chance has been waiting for you and you're late. I've been pacing the floor all day, and it was so good to see a human being. I just poured out my heart about Joey and cried all over Chance's sweater. Chance was very kind to me."

"And," Chance said, "we are going to find a solution to this mess. When two people love each other, nothing should stand in the way of their happiness. Right, Brooke?"

"I guess so."

"May I kiss you now?"

"No!"

"Why not?"

"Yeah," Julie said, "why not? Chance came straight from the airport to see you."

"And," he added, "I worked my little heart out to get that job done over there so I could get back here."

"I do believe," Julie said, much too loudly, "that I will walk into the kitchen and prepare a pot of coffee for us."

After Julie left the room, Chance chuckled softly and then walked to where Brooke stood.

"Brooke," he said quietly, "I am so incredibly glad to see you."

"Hello, Chance," she said, a lovely smile on her lips.

"Much, much better," he said, gathering her close and kissing her deeply.

Chance lifted his head and cupped Brooke's face in his hands. His blue eyes roamed over her soft curls, the freckles on her nose, her eyes and cheeks and chin, as if he were etching her features indelibly in his mind. Brooke gazed up at him, seeing the warmth, the tenderness in the sapphire pools, and her heart raced. Chance was home and Brooke was so very, very glad.

"Beebee," he said. "Nope. I'll call you Brooke. A brook has hidden treasures beneath its surface and more depth than meets the eye. I will definitely call you Brooke."

"I'm glad you're home, Chance."

"We have a problem."

"We do?"

"Julie and Joey. I'm telling you, Brooke, there has to be a way to help them solve this. Julie is really coming unglued, and I bet Rather is in no better shape. Aren't you going to take off your coat?"

"What? Oh, yes," she said, removing it and placing it on a chair. "I don't have any answers for them. Joey wants an old-fashioned family, and Julie has always dreamed of a modeling career."

"What do you want?"

"For them to be happy."

"No, I mean for yourself," Chance said, sitting on the sofa and patting the cushions next to him.

"Today," she said, sitting down beside him. "I just do one at a time."

"No hopes or dreams or fantasies?"

"No," she said softly.

"You're never too old to believe in Santa Claus, Brooke."

Brooke glanced up quickly and found Chance looking at her steadily. She knew what he was saying. *He* was Santa Claus, and he was asking her to trust and believe in him, accept all that he did and said as being honest and real.

"Don't say anything," he said, trailing his thumb over her cheek. "We'll do it your way for now. One day at a time."

"Can I come out now?" Julie called.

"Yes." Chance laughed. "I kissed Brooke and she passed out on the floor."

"Oh, shut up," Brooke said, poking him in the ribs.

"Coffee," Julie said, bringing in a tray.

"Are you all right, Julie?" Brooke asked.

"No, but you two have better things to do than worry about me. Oops, I hear the doorbell. If that's Joey, I'm going to cry again."

Julie answered the summons, and Joey Rather entered the living room. Introductions were made and the two men shook hands.

"Santa Claus, right?" Joey said.

"That's me," Chance said nodding.

"Tell you what, Santa," Joey said, "how about bringing me a tall, beautiful lady who will agree to marry me and have a houseful of kids?"

"Joey, don't," Julie said quietly.

"I'll see what I can do," Chance said.

"Hell, I'm sorry," Joey said. "I'm dumping on everyone. I don't even know why I'm here."

"Game isn't over until the last whistle blows," Chance said.

"Good point," Joey replied. "What do you think, Chance? Full court press?"

"Nope. Definitely calls for man-to-man, one-on-one with no time-outs."

"Huh?" Brooke said.

"You playing in my league?" Joey asked.

"Yeah, I sure am," Chance said. "I signed up so fast I didn't know what hit me."

"What?" Brooke and Julie said in unison.

"The opponents are worthy," Joey said. "Tough."

"Indeed they are," Chance said. "But, Joey, I intend to win."

"Awright!" Joey grinned. "We'll give 'em hell."

"Would you two speak English!" Brooke yelled.

"Certainly, my dear," Chance said, clearing his throat. "Joey and I were simply stating that we are embarking upon a tremendous undertaking that will utilize our entire capacity of stamina, intelligence and patience, but the final victory will be ours. Understand?"

"No."

"In short, Julie will marry Joey, and you, Brooke Bradley, will marry me!"

Four

___

I beg your pardon?'' Brooke asked, hardly above a whisper.

"I don't believe this," Julie groaned, sinking onto a chair.

"I'm hungry," Chance said. "Let's go eat."

"Good idea," Joey said. "Grab your coats, folks!"

"Not on your life, buster!" Julie said. "I want to know what's going on here. What are you and Chance up to?"

"Oops," Joey said. "Maybe we should double-date another time, Chance."

"Indeed," Chance agreed solemnly. "Hang in there, buddy."

Joey managed to stuff a sputtering Julie into her coat and hustle her out the door. Chance sat down next to Brooke on the sofa and gave her one of his most dazzling smiles.

"You really had me going there for a minute," Brooke said. "But I have it figured out now."

"Oh?"

"Sure. Joey was really depressed and possibly about to give up on Julie. So! You pretended to be in a similar situation so he wouldn't feel alone. Then! You equated it to an athletic challenge, which Joey can certainly relate to, and he's all charged up again and determined to win Julie's hand in marriage. That was very nicely done, Chance."

"Thank you. I thought it was pretty good, considering I was winging it off the top of my head. I..." Chance stopped speaking and frowned. "I'll be damned," he said slowly.

"What's wrong?"

"That spiel I rattled off to Joey. Brooke, I meant every word, I realize that now! I want a permanent future with you as much as Joey does with Julie! I've never had anything sneak up on me like this before. It's rather jarring, but it's fantastic, too. I should have known when I worked like a crazy man in San Diego so I could get home to you. Don't you see? I love you! I'm in love with you, Brooke Bradley."

"Oh, no, please don't say that," Brooke said, her hands flying to her cheeks. "What happened to I'm nice to be with?"

"Now, don't panic, okay? I realize my timing is not terrific because I have a long way to go before you really trust and believe in me. But, Brooke, I said I would always be honest with you, and realizing that I love you is just too big to keep from you. It isn't going to change anything for now, though. I won't rush you or ask more than you're willing to give."

"Oh, Chance, this is crazy!"

"No, it's great. I really like being in love. I've never done it before and it feels terrific. I meant it when I said I want to marry you, but I'll put that on the back burner for now. Hey, you're not going to have any curl left in your hair if you don't leave it alone. You're shook, huh?"

"You could say that, yes. People don't go from building snowmen together to getting married!"

"Why not? We'll do all the in-between stuff because I know you don't love me yet, but the end result will be the same. I just personally cut a few corners, that's all."

"How very efficient of you." Brooke frowned. "Your computer mind is working overtime."

"Yep. Let's go eat. I'm starving."

"I could use about six hot fudge sundaes."

"Oh, poor Brooke," he said, pulling her close. "I've really jangled your nerves. I didn't mean to," he said, tilting her chin up and lowering his lips onto hers.

Forget hot fudge sundaes, Brooke thought dreamily. Being kissed by Chance Tabor was all a person needed. Being held in those strong arms was soothing and... He loved her? Oh, good heavens, no!

"Chance," she said, pushing against his chest, "did you ever stop to consider that you only *think* you are in love with me? You said yourself that it's a new experience for you, and maybe you misread the signals."

"No way. I love you. Don't let that frighten you, Brooke. You probably feel like you're doing a déjà vu number with a guy declaring his love and then disappointing you. Well, I'm the real goods, babe. There is nothing phony going on here. You'll come to realize that, and I'll be a paragon of patience in the interim. Brooke, I really am going to pass out if I don't get some food."

"Oh, yes, of course, food."

Brooke vaguely remembered leaving the apartment and driving with Chance to a nearby steak house. Her mind was whirling from the impact of Chance's words, and she felt as if she were walking in a fog.

Chance Tabor said that he was in love with her, and that was the worst news flash of the year. She absolutely, positively did *not* want him to say that he loved her! Now she would be forced to make judgments and decisions she was ill equipped to do. She would have to somehow know if he was telling the truth, if his declarations and softly spoken words were valid, real. Oh, why did he have to ruin everything by announcing that he had fallen in love with her? She was enjoying his company, his kiss, his touch, the very essence of him so much, and now he'd gummed it up. Damn the man!

"Right?" Chance said.

"Pardon me?"

"I was just seeing if you were here and you're not. Brooke, you've got to calm down before you slip over the edge. You finished your dinner, and I'll bet you didn't taste a bite. I ordered you a hot fudge sundae. Maybe that will help."

"Thank you."

Chance did not speak while Brooke ate the gooey dessert down to the last lick of the spoon.

"Feeling better?" he asked.

"Much."

"Good, because I want to ask you something."

"Certainly. I'm totally under control. Do you think the effect hot fudge sundaes have on me is psychological?"

"Probably, but don't knock it if it works."

"So, what's the question you want to ask me?"

"Will you go away with me this weekend?"

"Oh, Lord," Brooke said, covering her face with her hands. "Tell me you didn't say that."

"Hey," he said, pulling her hands free, "it's important."

"To what? Your libido?"

"No! We have got to be together as much as possible and in varied circumstances and locations. You need to learn how trustworthy I am."

"Like a Boy Scout?"

"I wouldn't go that far. Will you do it?"

"I have to think, Chance. So much has happened, and I'm not sure how I feel about all this."

"Fair enough. You can tell me your decision tomorrow."

"So soon?"

"I thought we'd go to Aspen, and I need to make reservations for rooms. Please note the plural of the word room. That was rooms, my sweet. One for you and one for me."

"Which I'm sure is not your usual Aspen accommodations," Brooke said, frowning.

"My wanton ways are a thing of the past." Chance grinned. "We'll have a great time, you'll see."

"I don't know, Chance."

"Sleep on it. Speaking of which, I could use some shuteye myself. I've been operating on coffee and catnaps all weekend. I hate to take you home, though."

"You need your rest."

"I know, but I have this fear that, once you're alone, you'll come up with a hundred reasons why you shouldn't trust me. Do you suppose you could blank your mind until I see you tomorrow? No, I guess not. But, Brooke, don't cancel us out. Give us a chance."

Brooke looked into the blue pools of Chance's eyes and felt the familiar fluttering of her heart, the warmth of desire tingling throughout her. Oh, how easy it would be to throw up her hands in defeat and give in to the forces pulling at her senses. How simple it would be to silence the inner voice of warning and reach out to this man who caused such tempestuous emotions within her. But she couldn't and the reality of that fact brought a sad ache to her heart.

"There it is in your eyes," Chance said quietly, "that flicker of fear and sadness. It shouldn't be there, Brooke, and I intend to make it disappear forever. There will be only happiness there, and desire when I pull you into my arms. I love you, Brooke, and you're going to come to believe that."

"Chance, I . . ."

"I'll take you home," he said, smiling gently.

In Brooke's living room Chance kissed her deeply and then drew his fingers through her soft curls, watching them fall again to rest on her cheeks. He ran his hands down her arms to grasp her hands and bring each palm to his lips. Then in a low voice he said good night and left, shutting the door quietly behind him.

Brooke walked slowly to her room, wishing that Julie was home so that they could talk. Wishing that there was someone, anyone to speak to with the fervent hope of sorting through the jumble in her mind. Being close to Chance Tabor was foolhardy and dangerous, yet the thought of never seeing him again evoked a vision of loneliness, of empty hours.

When she was lying in bed, Brooke stared up into the darkness. She had met Chance when he was Santa Claus, she thought suddenly. He had been the fantasy symbol of the Christmas holiday, a make-believe figure that would disappear from thought and view when the festivities were over. What if she held fast to him for that long? Gave herself Chance Tabor, her Santa Claus, as a Christmas present? A lovely, warm, wonderful gift to herself for a short period of time. Instead of the bleak, empty Christmas that she was facing, she could share it with Chance.

And then? Then it would be back to reality, back to knowing he was out of her reach, for the doubts would return and with them her inability to decipher the truth. Was it unfair to Chance to play out a Christmas fantasy with him in the starring role? No, she'd made no promises, no pledges. She had the right, as he did, to conduct herself as she saw fit in their relationship.

Yes, she would do it! She would grab hold of a whiff of happiness, make memories of laughing, loving times and tuck them away in a treasured place in her heart and mind. She would be with Chance in the fairy-tale world that Christmas created, and when the holiday was over, she would once again face the facts as they truly were.

Brooke burrowed under the blankets and drifted off to sleep with a gentle smile on her lips. She did not stir until the shrill ringing of her alarm brought her from a deep, dreamless slumber. Her roommate was already in the kitchen when Brooke entered, and Julie placed two mugs of steaming coffee on the table.

"All I have to say is," Julie said, "your Chance and my Joey are a lethal combination. The two of them together are dangerous."

"Chance isn't exactly mine."

"Ha! Try telling *him* that."

"What happened with you and Joey last night?"

"Nothing. He was acting so weird that I stopped talking to him. He just smiled at me like a Cheshire cat and looked so darned pleased with himself he was driving me nuts. And you? You were asleep when I got home."

"Chance hadn't gotten much sleep in California so I was back here early. Julie, I've made a decision about Chance, but you mustn't tell Joey."

"My lips are sealed. What's up?"

"I'm giving myself Chance as a Christmas present, and then, when the holidays are over, I'll step back into reality."

"Huh? Goodness, for a minute there I thought you were serious."

"I am."

"You can't be! Beebee, that is the most ridiculous thing I've ever heard. You can't treat Chance like a sweater that doesn't fit and exchange him for something else the day after Christmas.''

"Julie, I have the right to do whatever I want. Other people in this world certainly do, including you. I don't intend to lie to Chance and say I'm making any long-term commitment to him. He has set ideas as to where our relationship is going and so do I. The fact that the ideas don't match isn't my fault.''

"But why? Why can't your reality be to stay with Chance? He's crazy about you, Beebee. Any idiot could tell that just by the way he looks at you.''

"Julie, I am still Brooke Bradley, remember? Dumb-dumb Brooke, who doesn't know the good guys from the bad. I'm giving myself this time with him without questioning his motives or actions or words. I'll be like Cinderella. After Christmas the fantasy will be over. The difference is that Cinderella knew her Prince Charming was on the level. I don't have the ability to figure out that kind of stuff. I'll have to be cautious again, taking one day at a time and preparing myself for whatever bad news that happens.''

"I'm hating this, Beebee. I really am. I like your Chance. Couldn't you be a little more open-minded about this? I think Chance is being totally honest with you.''

"No, because Chance is already saying things that should be making me run for the hills.''

"Like the little tidbit about your getting married?'' Julie laughed. "I nearly fainted.''

"See what I mean? He moves so fast, and under normal circumstances I'd be bailing out by now because I'd be in over my head. But with *my* plan, he can blither on about anything he pleases from now until Christmas because I know exactly what I'm doing for a change. I, Brooke Bradley, am controlling my own destiny.''

"And on December twenty-sixth you start examining Chance's motives again.'' Julie frowned. "It's cold.''

"It's realistic! And it's not dishonest or misleading or anything. Chance and I are on different wavelengths, that's all. Oh, Julie, all I'm asking for is a couple of weeks with a very nice man. Is that so wrong?"

"I guess not, but plans like this one have a way of backfiring. Look at the time! We're going to be late for work."

"Did I mention I'm going to Aspen with Chance for the weekend?" Brooke asked as she rose from the table and rinsed out her coffee cup. "Close your mouth, Julie. We're getting separate rooms."

"Chance agreed to separate rooms?"

"It was his idea."

"Strange. Very strange. You'd better stay alert, cookie."

"Fear not. I know exactly what I'm doing," Brooke said, lifting her chin and marching from the room.

"I think Marie Antoinette said that once," Julie muttered.

It was a sound, reasonable plan, Brooke decided firmly as she drove to work. She was long overdue for some sophistication in her life. There was something worldly about a short-term affair.

"Affair?" she said aloud. "Oh, now wait a minute." Affairs were a whole different ball game. They were sophistication to the max. Making love with Chance Tabor had not been penciled in on the list of activities for the next few weeks. But when one was controlling one's destiny, one could do anything one chose. But sleep with Chance Tabor? Be the recipient of all that masculinity, strength tempered with gentleness? "Goodness," Brooke said as fingers of desire danced through her, "I'd better think about something else. Whew!"

By late that afternoon Brooke could have eaten a dozen hot fudge sundaes without blinking an eye. She was a wreck! She knew beyond a shadow of a doubt that she could never make love with a man she didn't love. So, okay, she told herself, Chance was her Christmas present to herself, but it did not include going to bed with the man.

Granted, Chance was the best-looking, most blatantly masculine man she had ever met. And, yes, he was warm and dear and made her smile. She missed him terribly when he was gone, and her heart did a tap dance when he walked into the room. His eyes weren't mere eyes, they were sapphire pools of fathomless depths that made her tremble, and she adored his thick, wavy, dark hair that curled when it got wet. He evoked desires in her like none she had ever felt before, and being kissed by him and held in those strong arms was heaven itself. But she wasn't in love with him, for Pete's sake! So, therefore, lovemaking was not on the agenda.

"And *that* takes care of *that*," Brooke said as she drove home. "Everything is shipshape." Having control of one's life was a heady feeling. She didn't presume to push anyone's buttons, only her own. She wasn't being unfair to Chance by not telling him her plans. After all, he'd announced that they were to be married without consulting her. They were each doing their thing, and that was perfectly reasonable. Chance would have the choice of seeking greener pastures after Christmas when she refused to make a commitment to him, and Brooke would have had a glorious time in the interim without having to question his words and actions, which she was lousy at anyway. Yep, everything was going fine.

"Howdy-do," Brooke sang out cheerfully when she entered the apartment.

"Beebee!" Julie yelled, running out of the bedroom. "You won't believe this!"

"Slow down. What's wrong?"

"Nothing! Listen, Joey has a lot of connections with people from when he played basketball. He got me an interview with the head of a modeling agency in Los Angeles. Can you imagine? I'm leaving tonight!''

"But what about your job? Joey is helping you to further your career? This doesn't make sense.''

"I said my mother is sick, and my boss let me off.''

"Your nose is going to grow, Julie Mason. Why, pray tell, is Joey doing this? It's the exact opposite from what he wants.''

"He said he can't force me to marry him and have a baby. He wants me to have a chance at my modeling career before I settle down. Isn't he wonderful? Oh, I love him so much. I'm so excited. Come help me pack. Joey is taking me to the airport.''

An hour later Joey Rather arrived, and Brooke looked at him anxiously, searching his face for some clue as to what he was feeling.

"How's life?'' she said, squinting at him.

"Superb. How're things with you and Chance?''

"Joey, Julie is leaving for L.A.!''

"I know. I set it up, remember?''

"You're not playing with a full deck, Mr. Rather. She's off to the glamour and glitter, the big time, the wild parties. You're crazy!''

"We'll see,'' he said, smiling at her smugly.

"Goodbye,'' Julie said, dashing into the room and hugging Brooke. "I love you. I'll call you soon. Wish me luck. Bye.''

"Bye,'' Brooke said as they scooped up Julie's luggage and went out the door. "You're crazy, Joey Rather!''

Brooke was still frowning a few minutes later when Chance telephoned.

"Hi,'' he said after her hello.

"Chance, do you know what idiotic thing Joey did?''

"Yes.''

"You do?''

"Yes. Joey is a wise, wise man."

"Then you're both crazy."

"Time will tell, my sweet. So, did you think about the Aspen trip?"

"What? Oh, sure. I'd love to go."

"You would? Just like that?"

"Just remember I'm a lousy skier."

"You're really going to go?"

"Chance, would you prefer I said no? You're acting very strange."

"I'm in shock! I'm also thrilled out of my mind. This is fantastic! Okay, let me think. I've got to make the reservations and then burn the midnight oil to get this program written for the California outfit. I may not be able to see much of you for the rest of the week, but we'll make up for it at Aspen. I love you, Brooke."

"Well, I..."

"You don't have to answer when I tell you that. Just hear it, and little by little it will sink in as being the absolute truth. I intend to tell you I love you at every opportunity. Well, back to my floppy disks."

"Your who?"

"They're gizmos that go in disk drives on computers. Never mind. I'll call you tomorrow. I sure wish I could see you tonight, but duty calls. Miss me a bit, okay? Bye."

"Goodbye," she said, hanging up the receiver. Well, she'd done it. She'd agreed to go away with a man for the weekend. No, not just a man. Chance. What a shame that he was busy tonight. The apartment was all hers, and she could have fixed him a nice dinner. There were pretty candlesticks and candles in a cupboard somewhere, and Gran had a crochet tablecloth that she could have borrowed. Add quiet music, wine and... Ohhh, how romantic. Miss Chance? Heavens, she was nearly pining away.

Good thing I'm not in love with him, Brooke thought heading for the kitchen, or I'd really be miserable because he isn't here.

Brooke ate dinner, finished addressing her Christmas cards and then invited Gran over to watch a Clark Gable movie on television. The apartment had seemed suddenly too empty, which Brooke immediately decided was due to Julie's hasty departure. Gran was brought up to date on Julie's adventure, and the older woman nodded in approval.

"Always knew that Joey had a good head on his shoulders," Gran said. "That man is so tall it's a wonder he doesn't get nosebleeds just walking around. But he's smart, our Joey."

"Gran, isn't anyone paying attention?" Brooke said. "Joey just turned the love of his life over to the flash-and-dash world. Chance thought it was a smart move, too. I swear, what's wrong with you people?"

"Don't suppose you'd like to make small wager on the outcome, would you?" Gran cackled merrily.

"No way. The last time I gambled, I landed on Santa Claus's lap."

"Lucky you. How is Chance?"

"Oh, fine. We're going to Aspen for the weekend. Separate rooms, of course."

"How boring."

"Gran, shame on you!"

"I'm old, but I'm not dead. Chance is a very sexy man. I saw him in the hall, and I must say he does know how to fill out a pair of pants."

"Gran!"

"Oh, hush, silly girl. You sound like a prude. You need a man like Chance in your life. He has a lot more to offer than a Saint Bernard, that's for sure."

"Chance *is* in my life. I just told you we're going away for the weekend. We're going to have a lovely time together between now and Christmas."

"And then?"

"I'm not making a commitment to a long-term relationship with Chance," Brooke said quietly. "I just can't, Gran."

"Oh, honey, you are basing everything on that good-for-nothing Chuck Finley. You should judge Chance on his own merits."

"That's just it. I don't know how to judge him at all. Let's watch Clark Gable."

"You're making a mistake about Chance. To put a time limit on something like that is foolish."

"No, Gran, it's called survival. I have to do it this way. I really do."

The next day was quiet in the office, and thoughts of Chance buzzed through Brooke's mind. When he called late in the evening, he sounded tired.

"You're working too hard," Brooke said.

"Clearing the decks so we can escape to the slopes. Man, I want to see you so badly. I really do miss you."

"I . . . miss you, too," she said. "You can't get away even for a little while?"

"No, I'm really pushed here. Listen, we're on an eight o'clock plane Saturday morning."

"We're flying?"

"You bet. I'm not wasting four hours driving each way. I want to get up there and enjoy. Gotta run, but I'll call you tomorrow. Any news from Julie?"

"No, nothing. I suppose she's very busy."

"Yeah, I imagine she is. Bye for now. I love you, Brooke. Brooke Bradley, you I love. I, Chance Tabor, am wildly in love with you and your nine freckles."

"Good night, Chance," she said laughing. Oh, he was so dear. She just absolutely adored him. No, that wasn't really a good enough word. Cherished? Yes. Treasured? Yes. Loved? Good heavens, no! But, oh my, how she did miss Chance Tabor. It seemed like an eternity since he'd kissed and held her, since she'd filled her senses with his special aroma and been aware of the desire he evoked surging through her. She wanted the remaining hours of the week to disappear in a puff of smoke and bring Chance and their magical weekend into the here and now. Because...she missed him.

The telephone calls from Chance on Thursday and Friday were brief. He sounded thoroughly exhausted and at one point lost track of what he was saying. He told Brooke that he would pick her up at seven on Saturday morning. Before she could express concern over the way he was pushing himself, he had said good night and hung up.

Brooke packed her suitcase Friday night except for last-minute items and went to bed early. She was an amalgam of emotions—excited, nervous and also worried about Chance's health. She wanted only to sleep so the morning would come and with it Chance Tabor.

Brooke woke even before the alarm sounded and hurried to the bathroom to shower and shampoo her hair. With her curls blown dry into a soft halo around her head, she dressed in lavender wool slacks and a lavender ski sweater with a mountain scene knitted across the bodice.

Her heart was racing, and there was a smile on her face when she answered Chance's knock at the door.

And then she was in his arms. Before she had even realized she had done it, she had flung herself into his embrace and was caught against his hard chest by muscle-corded arms. Chance claimed her mouth in a feverish, urgent kiss that she answered in kind, savoring each sensation that rocketed through her.

Oh, yes, oh, yes, she had missed Chance Tabor!

"Hello, Brooke," Chance said, taking a ragged breath.

"Oh, Chance, you look so tired. Maybe we shouldn't go. You should rest."

"I'll take a nap later. I'm fine really. Oh, it's good to see you," he said, kissing her again until Brooke's knees began to tremble.

Chance lifted his head and swallowed heavily as he moved Brooke gently away from his body by gripping her shoulders. He stared at the floor for a moment, as if striving for control, and then looked at her, his blue eyes smoky with fatigue and desire. Neither spoke; they simply stood there drinking in the sight, the aroma, the very essence of the other.

There was a tension virtually crackling in the air, an element of heightened awareness of something new and different that somehow hadn't been there before. Seconds passed as their gazes held, and then Brooke slowly lifted her hand and placed it gently on Chance's cheek. His jaw tightened slightly at the feathery touch, and then with a quiet moan he pulled her to him and buried his face in her hair.

"Brooke" was all he said, and to her it was a celebration of sound.

Brooke seemed to float back from a faraway place as the euphoric glow slowly dissipated. But it left her with a smile on her lips and a honeyed warmth that consumed her from head to toe.

"We'd better go, Brooke," he said. "We don't want to miss our plane."

"I'm ready," Brooke answered, and they left the apartment and drove out to the airport.

No sooner had they fastened their seat belts on the plane, then Chance put his head back and fell sound asleep. Brooke smiled at his handsome profile and busied herself reading the magazines that had been stored in the pocket of the seat in front of her.

One brochure stated that Aspen had been founded over one hundred years before by prospectors mining silver. Now skiing was the attraction in the form of three mountains within a twelve-mile radius—Aspen, Buttermilk and Snowmass. Brooke had visited the town of Aspen and had been enthralled with the quaint shops and Victorian streets lined with old-fashioned streetlights. And this time she was going there with Chance.

"Oh, man," Chance said when the flight attendant's voice announcing their arrival woke him, "I didn't mean to leave you alone to stare out the window, Brooke."

"I'm glad you slept. Do you feel better?"

"Yeah, just a little groggy. The mountain air will wake me up in a hurry."

Aspen. It was a beehive of activity and a fairyland of snow. It was brightly colored skiing outfits, laughter dancing through the clear, cold air and people of every age, shape and size. Brooke felt a tingle of excitement shiver along her spine, and she smiled up at Chance, who returned the expression.

Chance had made reservations at a quaint hotel off the main street that was fashioned after a Swiss chalet. They had the promised separate rooms with a connecting inner door, and after unpacking, they headed out to explore the shops. Brooke declared firmly that Chance should go skiing and she would occupy her time. He flatly refused, saying he might go the next morning but that today was theirs. He wanted to be with her, he had stated softly, and Brooke thought that that was an absolutely lovely thing to say. They spent hours wandering through the shops, then sat on the outdoor balcony of a hotel and sipped hot cider as they watched the skiers coming down from the distant slopes.

"Oh, what a perfect day," Brooke said.

"Yep." Chance nodded. "I really like to come here. It's like being on another planet, and I need a break once in a while."

"You do work awfully hard, Chance."

"Building your own company from the ground up isn't easy, but we have a good solid reputation now for producing accurate programs on time. Your nose is pink from the cold. It's cute."

"How did my nose get into this conversation?" Brooke laughed.

"I'd like to spend hours talking about you. I want to know everything. Were you always so feminine, or did you have a tomboy stage? What's your favorite color? Do you like ketchup on your French fries, and who's your heart-throb movie star? Every detail, big and small, Brooke, because it's all a part of you and I love you."

Somewhere in the middle of Chance's parlance, his voice had dropped an octave. He had reached for Brooke's hand and was drawing a lazy circle in her palm with his thumb. The blue of his eyes was so sparkling clear that she felt as though she could see into the very recesses of his soul, and a tiny portion, a mere fraction of her mind, believed . . . that he loved her.

And she was scared to death. It had begun. The chipping away of her resolve and firm intention to never again trust her own judgment regarding the honesty of a man had begun. Chance Tabor had lifted the chisel in his hand and wielded the stroke that would be her eventual destruction. His softly spoken words, his steady gaze that held her immobile, were as powerful as a mighty blow.

She couldn't, wouldn't allow this to happen. These numbered days were to have been spent in blissful oblivion. And there was more, much more, that she must guard against. She must not, even for a fleeting second, examine her own emotions in regard to Chance Tabor. Strange and wondrous things were beginning to happen to her when he kissed and held her, touched her. She wanted to sing aloud at the sound of his laughter and drink in the sight of his beautiful face. She wanted... No! Neither her inner voice nor Chance's spoken words would be heeded.

"Brooke? You've gone away from me," Chance said quietly.

"What? Oh, I'm sorry."

"All this fresh air can get to you. Would you like to rest before dinner?"

"Yes, I think that's a good idea."

They walked to the hotel in silence with Chance's arm encircling Brooke's shoulders. She saw the appreciative glances he received from passing women, but he seemed oblivious to their scrutiny. He simply kept Brooke tightly by his side as if announcing she was his, and she shivered slightly.

In her room Chance opened the connecting door as he prepared to leave. "You take a nap," he said. "I'll wake you later. Is anything wrong besides being tired? You're awfully quiet."

"I wish you wouldn't say that you love me, Chance," Brooke said, sinking onto the edge of the bed.

"Why, Brooke? Because you still think I'm stringing you along? Or could it be because you're starting to believe in me?"

"Chance, don't."

"Damn it, Brooke," he said, sitting down next to her. "Look at me. Look into my eyes and see the truth. I love you! I love you with every breath in my body. Don't be afraid of me, but even more, don't be afraid of yourself. The past is gone, forgotten. The future could be ours, together, if you'd only let it be. Oh, yes, I love you, and I'm going to keep on saying it. I love your curls and your nine freckles. I love your smile and the soft velvet of your lips

and the way your body fits next to mine. All of you, head to
toe, inside and out, including your wacky hot fudge sundaes, I love.''

Chance got to his feet and stared down at her. Brooke
lifted her head to gaze up at him, and his jaw tightened as
he saw the tears shimmering in her eyes.

"Ah, Brooke, don't cry," he said, his voice raspy.
"There's no room for tears in the world we're creating, only
smiles. Hey, I'm Santa Claus, remember? I'm magic. I can
grant your fondest wish, make your dream come true. But
Brooke, you have to know what it is you want because I
missed the North Pole training course on mind reading. I
can only pray that, when you get in touch with yourself,
you'll decide that what you want for Christmas is me. Me,
Brooke, for a lifetime of Christmases."

"Oh, Chance."

"Rest. I'll see you later," he said, walking into his room
and closing the connecting door.

It seemed to take the last ounce of Brooke's strength to
remove her coat and tug off her shoes. A sob caught in her
throat and tears slid silently down her cheeks as she crawled
beneath the bedspread and curled into a ball.

She shut her eyes and saw only Chance's face. As she
opened them again, his image was still there, smiling tenderly at her, beckoning with a clearly spoken message from
the sapphire depths of his eyes to come to him.

Brooke rolled onto her back and stared at the ceiling,
searching deep within herself for answers, for a direction.
A fog seemed to float across her mental view of Chance,
shrouding him in a cloak of doubt. The insidious forces of
the past hammered at her, screamed of her flaw, her inability to know truth from fantasy. Chance grew smaller and
smaller, was whisked away by the cloud, and Brooke was left
with only herself.

And then a strangled sob escaped from her throat. There was nowhere to run, nowhere to hide from the discovery, from the voice that spoke from her heart and soul and mind.

She was in love with Chance Tabor.

Five

___

Brooke drew a shuddering breath and pressed her finger-tips to her aching temples. What was she going to do? Oh, what in heaven's name was she going to do? She had fallen in love with Chance Tabor, and she had never in her life been so miserable. Chance was, on the surface, everything that she could have ever wanted in a man. Everything.

If only she could stop right there, just throw caution to the winds, declare her love and receive Chance into her embrace. But she couldn't; she knew it, and that knowledge brought fresh tears to her eyes. She loved him, pure and simple, but beyond that was a sea of confusion. Chance was still shrouded in the cloak of doubt. He spoke such loving words, smiled so tenderly, but where was the truth? How did she know what was real?

And so now what? Did she pack her suitcases and slink away like the coward she was? Or did she hold fast to her whimsical plan to share a blissful Christmas with Chance?

She had pushed her own buttons and hit the wrong ones. She was on a destruction course, nothing could change it, and it was her fault, per usual. She was brilliant Brooke, who had no business playing grown-up games of love and lovers.

Lovers? She had firmly dismissed the possibility of making love with Chance because her feelings had not run that deeply. But now she had to leave with only the memories of the following days. She had to, for she still did not know his true motivations, nor would she ever have the wisdom to discover them. Any thoughts of staying with Chance after Christmas would have to be forgotten because she'd lost control of her emotions. She would hold fast to her gift, her Chance, and cherish each moment they shared.

Would that include the giving of herself to this man? She didn't know yet, but if the time came when it was right and good, she would not deny her inner desires.

Brooke gave way to the fatigue that claimed her and welcomed the peacefulness of sleep.

"Hey, sleepy girl," Chance said. "Can I tempt you with some dinner?"

"What?" Brooke said, slowly opening her eyes. "Oh, you're all dressed and ready to go."

"No rush. Tell you what. I'll meet you in the lobby whenever you're ready. There's a nice restaurant here so don't bother with your coat."

"Fine."

"You sleep cute." He smiled and then kissed her on the end of her nose. "I'll see you downstairs," he said, striding from the room.

Chance had dressed in black slacks and a bulky knit off-white fisherman's sweater that made his shoulders appear wide and strong. A mental vision of the ever-so-willing women that might be gathered below flashed before Brooke's eyes, and she scrambled off the bed.

For now, by gum, Chance Tabor was hers!

Brooke showered quickly and pulled on kelly-green slacks with a green-and-white striped sweater. She flicked her curls around her cheeks and applied a rosy lip gloss. Why she should be in such a terrific mood when her life was definitely in the blender she didn't know. It was probably because she was living out a fantasy, and gloomy words were taboo in fantasies, she thought ruefully. She, Brooke Bradley, was in love with Santa Claus and make-believe couldn't get better than that. She would reenter her oblivious state in regard to Chance and let nothing he said or did upset her mental equilibrium. She was going to enjoy.

Chance was indeed standing and talking to two attractive women when Brooke entered the lobby, and she walked over to the trio, slipping her arm through Chance's.

"Hello," she said ever so sweetly to the women.

"Don't worry, honey," the blond one said. "He made it very clear that he was waiting for you. Some people get all the luck. See ya."

Chance chuckled as Brooke waggled her fingers at the retreating females.

"See how scary you are?" he said.

"You betcha. Let's eat."

If Chance was surprised by the return of Brooke's good spirits, he made no mention of it. They chatted easily, comfortably, while they ate platters of seafood. They exchanged childhood tales and adventures of their painful adolescence. It was a fun time, a sharing time, a special time.

Each instant that Brooke raised her eyes to look at Chance, the realization of her love for him struck her once again. He was now an extension of her being, the other half of her self. She refused to think about the future.

"Chance," she said thoughtfully as they sipped after-dinner coffee, "why did Joey ship Julie off to Los Angeles? I seem to be the only one who thinks it was a dumb thing to do. Even Gran, our neighbor across the hall, was all enthused."

"Julie has a dream of being a model, but all she's done is one fashion show at a country club and a thirty-second spot on television for hand lotion. Joey gave me all this data when we talked."

"I see." Brooke smiled.

"Well, Joey didn't know diddly about modeling, either, so he called this buddy of his who owns an agency in L.A. and got the scoop. Let me tell you, Brooke, it is one tough career. There's hours and hours under the lights, wearing the wrong clothes in opposite seasons, never being able to eat enough to feed a bird, and on it goes. Joey is gambling on the fact that Julie will come to realize that it's not the life she wants and will come home to him."

"Risky, very risky."

"Maybe, but then love is worth taking risks for, don't you think? Joey is laying it all on the line and holding his breath. The battle he's fighting is against Julie's dream. Mine? I'm boxing at shadows, ghosts, in your mind. I intend to win, Brooke. I love you, and I want to spend the rest of my life with you. I wish I could feed that info into one of my computers and produce a printout to show me how I'm going to get you to believe me. I think I'm making a little progress, but I'm not sure. Brooke, what is it going to take to convince you to trust me?"

Brooke's dark eyes appeared as wide as saucers as she looked at Chance, and her voice was hushed when she spoke.

"It would really help if you were a direct descendant of Pinocchio," she said, "and your nose would grow if you lied. Or maybe if you really were Santa Claus because Santa Claus is a very trustworthy person. But, Chance, you're just a man, a human being. The problem isn't with you, it's me.

It's hopeless, it really is. I have no faith in my ability to know what is real. You'd be much better off if you just forgot you ever met me.''

"I can't do that," he said quietly. "You look so frightened, like a little girl. Do I cause that fear in your eyes?''

"I'm afraid of myself, me. It has nothing to do with you.''

"Yes, it does because you won't let me near you. Brooke, you must trust me a little, or you wouldn't have come away with me like this. That's a start, a good one. And each time I kiss you, you give more of yourself. When I walked into your apartment this morning, I could tell you had missed me as much as I did you. Can you deny that?''

"No. I did miss you. Oh, Chance, when I push the doubts away, you are so special, and you make me feel wonderful and cherished. I can hardly wait to see you after you've been away from me, and I love you so much. Oh, dear heaven," Brooke whispered, "what have I done?''

"You said you love me," Chance said, a wide smile spreading over his face. "You did! You love me? Are you in love with me?''

"No. Well, it doesn't matter because—''

"Doesn't matter? Brooke, this is the greatest day of my life! Talk about a Christmas present! Your love is the most fantastic gift I've ever received.''

"Chance, no! It doesn't change anything. We're not going to even be together after—''

"Not together after what?''

"Christmas. Chance, I didn't want to give you up yet so I gave you to myself as a Christmas present. I planned to have this time with you and not question your motives or actions or words. I just wanted to be with you. I loused it up, as usual, and fell in love with you. But later I'll have to face the fact that nothing has changed.''

"So on the day after Christmas I get the brush-off?''

"Well, sort of. I mean, I have no choice. Maybe it was selfish of me and I'll understand if you want to end it right now."

"I've never been a Christmas present before," he said, smiling. "And since your love is *my* gift, I'd better stick around. Besides, I am a representative of Santa Claus, and I'm on duty until the big day. I guess you're stuck with me through Christmas."

"Even though you know it's over afterward?"

"I'm computing all the facts, Miss Bradley," he said, tapping his temple with his finger. "I understand perfectly. Oh, and I love you, love you, love you. I figure I can say that as often as I please, right? Everything is out in the open now, and we can do whatever feels good during these days we have together. We each have our gift, and we should enjoy it to the fullest. Okay?"

"I think I'm getting confused," Brooke said, frowning.

"It's simple. If I got a toy fire engine for Christmas, it would be mine to do with as I chose. If I wanted to pull off all the wheels, I could. Or I could wash and polish it, whatever. You, your love, is my gift. I am yours. You can hand me over to that blonde in the tight pants or keep me for yourself. I'm in your hands for safekeeping until Christmas and you are in mine. That's how gifts work. They're given, no strings attached."

"I'm definitely confused."

"You'll see how it's going to work. Now! For example, I am going to take my present into the other room for some dancing in the glow of the firelight. Sound reasonable?"

"Yes, I guess so."

"And, of course, you'll have the opportunity to make some decisions regarding what you want to do with me."

"Well, I'm sure not giving you to that blond floozy!"

"That's comforting. She wasn't my type. That redhead over there isn't too bad."

"Forget it!"

"Okay—" he shrugged "—it's all up to you. Whatever you say, ma'am. I am totally at your disposal. I plan to take my role as a Christmas present very seriously, and you will have my complete cooperation. Shall we dance?"

"All right."

Brooke waited while Chance signed the receipt for dinner and then allowed him to lead her from the restaurant.

Had any of that conversation come even remotely close to making sense? she thought, shaking her head slightly. One thing was for sure. She could qualify for the Blabbermouth of the Year award. There she had sat, blithering away like a loony tune telling Chance that she loved him. But then what had happened? He'd sort of pulled back, regrouped and decided everything was hunky-dory. She was his Christmas present and he was hers. And he was agreeing to saying goodbye on December twenty-sixth? Yes, he'd said that he'd understood the plan. But . . . what did Chance Tabor intend to do with his Christmas present?

The room they entered was large, and many people were milling around. It had an intimate atmosphere because of a roaring fire in a huge stone fireplace and candles set on small tables. There was a dance floor beyond the carpeted area, and an abundance of deep cushioned sofas and chairs. Chance acknowledged a greeting from across the room with a nod of his head but made no attempt to join the people that he obviously knew. Instead, he led Brooke to the dance floor to dance to a slow song that was being played by a three-piece band.

Chance pulled Brooke tightly into his arms and moved her across the floor with an athletic gracefulness. Brooke stiffened slightly as she became acutely aware of his rugged length, his special male aroma and the heat emanating from his body.

"Relax, Brooke," he said quietly. "Relax and enjoy."

Oh, what the heck, why not? Brooke thought as she leaned against him. She was perfectly safe there in that crowded room. Good heavens, Chance felt good and smelled good, and she loved him so much. So very, very much. He was absolutely the most wonderful Christmas present that she had ever had.

"You feel so right close to me like this," Chance murmured in her ear. "It is definitely helpful that it's so dark in here. You are having a tremendous effect on me, Brooke."

Brooke's eyes widened as she felt the evidence of Chance's arousal pressing against her. As she attempted to pull away, he drew her closer, flattening his hand on her back and crushing her breasts against his chest. Brooke's cheeks became flushed and warm as desire started deep within her and moved unchecked throughout her. It spread with a sweet honeyed warmth, awakened her femininity and wreaked havoc with her sense of reality and reason. She was being swept away on a magic carpet while being held safely in the arms of the man she loved.

Brooke sighed with a soft sound of contentment, causing her breasts to move over Chance's chest. She heard his sharp intake of breath and felt his manhood stir against her.

"I'm dying," he growled.

"Then don't hold me so tightly," she whispered.

"I want to. You feel so great. But, oh, I really am dying. There should be a law against what you do to me."

"Maybe it's all in your head," Brooke said with a giggle.

"That's not the location of my problem." He chuckled. "Let's see here. I'll think about something else. What is your opinion of the state of the economy?"

"It's inflated," Brooke said, a bubble of laughter escaping from her lips. "These are *hard* times."

"You're killing me, lady," Chance moaned, moving her away from him.

"Sorry, sir. I'll try to control myself."

"Ah, Brooke—" he smiled, kissing her on the forehead "—I love to hear you laugh. It's a joyous sound, like the bells on a Santa's sleigh. Would you like to go sit by the fire and have a drink?"

"Yes, fine."

"Good. I don't think I could survive another dance with you."

"Thanks a bunch."

"Actually, that was a compliment, my sweet. You have very potent power for such a small person. Go sit on that sofa, and I'll forge my way through the masses to the bar."

"Remember, Chance," she smiled. "The redhead is a no-no."

"Check."

A couple vacated the sofa next to the hearth just as Brooke approached, and she smiled her thanks as she sank onto the plush cushion. The man nodded at her absently and redirected his attention to the woman at his side as they moved away. Brooke watched them leave, saw the readable messages of desire dance between their eyes, the knowing smiles tug at their lips. They were in love and didn't care if the world knew it. They no doubt trusted, believed, in each other with no questions asked, no reservations.

Oh, what sweet bliss it would be to love Chance like that, Brooke thought, to build a future, hold fast to the joy of sharing with another until death parted them. It was as though there was a dark, empty space within her, mocking, cold, screaming her inadequacy, her flaw.

How simple it sounded. Get to know, understand, trust and believe in Chance Tabor. Hear the words he spoke so gently and cherish, not question, them. Look into his crystal-blue eyes and drink in the sight of the warmth and tenderness directed at her. Savor his kiss and touch as the first of millions to come during their eternity together. Love him—heart, mind, body and soul. Forever. How simple it

Say yes to free gifts worth over $20.00

Say yes to a rendezvous with romance, and you'll get 4 classic love stories—FREE! You'll get an elegant manicure set—FREE! And you'll get a delightful surprise—FREE! These gifts are worth over $20.00—but you can have them without spending even a penny!

MONEY-SAVING HOME DELIVERY!

Say yes to Silhouette romances and you'll enjoy the convenience of previewing brand-new books every month, delivered right to your home before they appear in stores. Each book is yours for only $1.95—30¢ less than the retail price.

SPECIAL EXTRAS—FREE!

You'll get your free monthly newsletter, packed with news on your favorite writers, upcoming books, even recipes from your favorite authors.

Say yes to a Silhouette love affair. Complete, detach and mail your Free Offer Card today!

Silhouette Desire®
FREE OFFER CARD

4 FREE BOOKS

AN ELEGANT MANICURE SET

Place YES
Sticker here

PLUS A SURPRISE BONUS

Please send me my 4 Silhouette Desire novels, free, along with my free manicure set and surprise bonus gift. Then send me 6 new books every month, as they come off the presses, and bill me just $1.95 per book (30¢ less than retail), with no extra charges for shipping and handling. If I am not completely satisfied, I may return a shipment and cancel at any time. The free books and gifts remain mine to keep!

CYD126

Name_____
(PLEASE PRINT)

Address_____ Apt._____

City_____

Prov./State_____ Postal/Code/Zip_____

sounded. How impossible it was, for she didn't trust in her instincts to know the truth when spoken by a man.

Each separate facet of Chance was perfection itself, but blended together he was a man, total, complete. Brooke lacked that inborn womanly sense of understanding about men. She had been completely wrong about Chuck Finley, couldn't comprehend why her father placed his work before the importance of his daughter, thought Joey Rather was a dumb-dumb when everyone else considered his plan regarding Julie brilliant and... and Chance? Chance Tabor could be acting out his routine seduction plan for all she knew. She could be just one more in an endless string of women who fell prey to his charisma, looks and nonstop body. He could be nibbling on that redhead's ear right now, and she'd be none the wiser. He wouldn't dare! That rat! She'd—

"Made it," Chance said, sitting down next to her and handing her a drink.

"Get lost?"

"It's crowded up there, plus I had two offers for my body."

"I knew it!" Brooke said, taking a deep swallow of her drink and nearly choking.

"I was kidding! Easy on that stuff, it's potent. Actually, I had *three* offers for my body."

"You're a dead person, Tabor."

"Oh, man," he said with a laugh, "you're so cute when you're jealous. It does great things for my ego, you know what I mean? Even your nine freckles look fierce."

"You're crazy," Brooke said, smiling, "and I... Well..."

"Say it, Brooke," he said softly. "Say that you love me. Please let me hear it again. You and those words are my Christmas present, remember?"

"I do love you, Chance," she whispered. "I wish so much that I was someone else, someone different than who I am. I wish—"

"Chance!" a voice boomed. "How in the hell are you, man?"

"Patrick!" Chance said, getting up and shaking hands with a handsome blond man. "Where's Susie?"

"She's calling home to check with the baby sitter."

"Patrick, meet Brooke. Brooke, this ugly lug is one of the sharpest computer guys in the state."

"Hello." Brooke smiled.

"Hi, gorgeous," Patrick said. "Hey, Chance, I went to a convention last week and saw some software that you wouldn't believe. Sit down. I've got to tell you about a database program that is unreal. You can produce a spread sheet that . . ."

Brooke plastered a pleasant expression on her face and tuned out the conversation that didn't make any sense. The warmth from the fire made her thirsty, and she finished her drink in two swallows, her eyes watering slightly at the bitter taste. Patrick droned on about RAM and ROM, and Chance seemed to be hanging on to every word.

Men and their toys, Brooke thought, dreamily, staring into the leaping flames. Goodness, she was sleepy, and there was such a strange buzzing noise in her ears. Like funny little bees. Did bees have knees? Didn't anyone care if bees had knees? Poor bees. Her head was heavy, so heavy. Would Chance mind if she just sort of leaned it on his shoulder for a second? Just for a second?

"Uh-oh," Chance said as Brooke's head landed with a thud on his shoulder.

"You got a problem?" Patrick asked.

"Hey, sleepy girl," Chance said. "Brooke?"

"Hmmm?"

"Fresh air, booze and the fire," Chance said. "You've had the course, kid. Come on."

"Hmmm?"

"See ya, Patrick." Chance chuckled, scooping Brooke into his arms. "Tell Susie hello for me."

The crowd waved good-naturedly as Chance made his way across the room with Brooke nestled in his arms.

"Do . . . bees . . . have knees?" she mumbled.

"I'll do an in-depth study on it, babe." He laughed, causing her head to bob up and down on his chest.

"Thank you. I'd really 'preciate that."

"My Brooke is blitzed," he said, smiling as he went up the stairs.

Outside her room Chance set Brooke on her feet and circled her shoulders with his arm as he reached in her pocket for her key. Then she was airborne again and a moment later was deposited on the bed. Brooke popped back up the moment Chance laid her down and blinked her eyes.

"Is it morning?" she said.

"No, you phased out by the fire. Here, let me take off your shoes. How do you feel?"

"I'm okay, I think. It was just so warm and I could swear I had a dream about bees."

"Do you think you can get undressed?" Chance said, sitting down next to her.

"Why?" she said, squinting at him.

"So you can go to sleep. I'm not trying to seduce you here." He smiled.

"Oh. Well, sure, I can get my nightie on. I really am okay now."

"Yeah, you seem all right. I guess that fire and the drink just got to you for a minute."

"I'm sorry if I embarrassed you in front of Patrick."

"Of course you didn't. Patrick thinks I'm a lucky man, and I am. I'd like to kiss you now, Brooke. I believe a person should always kiss their Christmas present good-night, don't you?''

"Well, then I should kiss you, too, because you're *my* present.''

"Makes perfect sense to me," he said, gathering her into his arms and claiming her mouth.

The kiss was sensuous and soft and tasted like rum. The kiss was a meeting of tongues and a rising of passions an instant after it began. The kiss was ecstasy, and Brooke voiced no objection as Chance pushed her gently back onto the pillow.

In a fluid motion he swung around and stretched out next to her, pinning her legs with one of his as his tongue delved deep into the darkness of her mouth. His hand slid under the waistband of her sweater to move to one breast, stroking the nipple into a taut bud with his thumb.

Brooke welcomed the sensations swirling within her and welcomed the weight of Chance's body. His arousal was evident, pressing against her, announcing his need, his want of her. She sank her hands into his thick, wavy hair to bring his mouth harder onto hers and heard his breathing grow raspy.

"Brooke," he said, lifting his head a fraction, "let me see you. Please, babe, I just want to see you, touch you."

Brooke consented by actions, not words, as she moved her arms to allow him to pull the sweater over her head and then remove the wispy material of her bra. She heard his sharp intake of breath as he gazed at her breasts, and his hand was trembling as he reached tentatively to fill his palm with the soft flesh.

"You're so lovely," he said, his voice hushed. "Perfect. Your breasts are like beautiful flowers, so smooth, firm. Mine. You're mine."

Chance lowered his head to draw one rosy bud into his mouth as his thumb trailed over the other. Brooke gasped as the sensations rocketed through her. His mouth on her breast was causing a sweet pain in the lower regions of her body, in the secret places of her femininity. Deep, deep within her the flame burst into a raging fire of passion like none she had ever known before.

Chance gave loving attention to her other breast, and a soft moan escaped Brooke's throat. He took possession of her mouth again in a feverish kiss as his manhood pressed hard against her, declaring a promise of what could be hers.

"Brooke," Chance said, taking a ragged breath, "I want to feel your hands on me. I need your touch."

"Yes," she said and missed him the moment he moved to draw his sweater over his head and drop it onto the floor. "Oh," she said, a look of wonder and awe on her face as her eyes roamed over the dark hair on his chest.

She reached out her hand to place it on the muscled wall, sinking her fingertips into the curly mass. She felt Chance tremble under her feathery foray and heard the quiet moan in his throat as she caressed the buttons of his nipples.

"You have the touch of an angel," he said as he moved closer to her to cover her mouth with his.

His chest brushed her breasts, and she slid her hands around to rest on his back, feeling the muscles bunch and move. He was so strong, so powerful, yet Brooke somehow knew that he would consume her with an infinite gentleness. He would think not only of his needs but of hers as well. With all the doubts that tormented her, she couldn't fathom why she knew with such crystal clarity that their union would be a celebration of mutual giving and taking. But it would be ecstasy.

Because, oh, yes, she did want him to make love to her. It would be yet another glorious part of her Christmas present. He would be hers in the greatest intimacy between man and woman. Her man, his woman, their gift to the other to cherish for as long as each chose to hold fast to the memory.

"Brooke, oh, my Brooke," Chance said. "I want you so much. So much."

Brooke looked into the sapphire pools of Chance's eyes, which were almost smoky gray with desire. She saw the tight set of his jaw and felt the tremor sweep through his body as he strove for control. Before she could speak, he turned and sat on the edge of the bed and reached for his sweater, only to have it hang limply from his hands. Resting his elbows on his knees, he bent his head and drew a shuddering breath.

Brooke placed her hand on his back, but he jerked away from her touch. Without looking at her, Chance handed her sweater to her.

"Cover yourself," he said quietly.

"Why, Chance?"

"I can't take any more right now. I want you too badly, and if I touch you again, I won't be able to stop. I said I wouldn't seduce you and I won't, I swear it. But I ache for you, Brooke. I'm going to my room now. Are you all right?"

"No."

"What's wrong?" he said, turning quickly to look at her. "Damn it, I'm a man, not a saint."

"And I'm a woman, not a child!"

"Meaning?"

"You continually make decisions for me. That's fine to a point because I am your Christmas present. But so far all I've done is tell you to keep your paws off the redhead. Chance, would you feel used, cheapened in some way, if I said I wanted you to make love to me as part of my gift? Is that asking too much? Because if it is, I'll understand. It won't change the outcome of our relationship, but I do want you and I don't even know if that's fair. Oh, dear, I'm going to cry in about two seconds so say no without yelling your head off and then go away."

Brooke gathered her sweater into a bundle and covered her breasts, then shut her eyes and swallowed the lump in her throat. Chance didn't speak and a tension grew in the silence. She wanted to peer at him from beneath her lashes to see his face, gauge his expression to what she had said, but didn't have the courage.

She'd never in her life done anything so bold, rash. It was so far removed from her code of conduct that it was absurd and she didn't care. She wanted Chance Tabor to make love to her. Pure and simple. She wanted him. And if he rejected her, she was absolutely going to die!

"Do you realize what you're saying, doing?" Chance finally said.

"Yes," she said, slowly opening her eyes. "But if you don't—"

"Don't want you? You know how much I do, and, no, I won't feel used, I'll feel honored. But, Brooke, you have to understand something. We can mutually agree to take this step and share a beautiful, wondrous experience. Our emotional reactions, however, can't be predetermined, and we'll have to be responsible for our own. Agreed?"

"Yes."

"That gives us each license to place whatever meaning, whatever importance, on our coming together. Why am I saying all this to you? Because I am about to make love with the only woman I have ever, and will ever, love. I will never, *never*, Brooke, forget this night."

Tears clung to Brooke's lashes as she listened to Chance's softly spoken words, and her heart nearly burst with love for him. She refused to think beyond the moment, to examine or challenge anything that was taking place. There was no world beyond this room, no tomorrows, no worries or doubts or fears. There was only... Brooke's Chance.

Chance picked up her hand and kissed the palm, then placed it on his heart, gazing at Brooke in a timeless moment before once more stretching out next to her. She welcomed him back into her embrace as she pushed the sweater away to leave no barrier between the heat of their skin. Her breasts grew taut as they brushed against his chest hair, and she arched her back to fully receive each sensation.

In a lambent journey of exploration and discovery, Chance kissed and caressed her with a maddening, tantalizing slowness. Inch by glorious inch he drew her slacks and panties down her slender legs, kissing her velvet softness as it came into his smoldering view. Her passion soared and she moved restlessly, seeking more, wanting more, but still Chance held back, his arms trembling as he supported his weight above her.

"You're so beautiful," he said, his eyes roaming over her naked splendor.

"I want you so much, Chance."

He left her for a moment to rid himself of his clothing, his perfectly proportioned body glistening in the glow of the lamp. His manhood was strong, ready to consume her, fill her, and she needed the fulfillment that he promised. Now.

"Please," she whispered.

He covered her body with his and took her mouth in a feverish kiss. Her hands roamed over his back feeling the muscles, the power and strength of his rugged frame. Chance parted her legs with his knee to move to just beyond her femininity and then he hesitated.

"Say it, Brooke," he said, his voice raspy. "Say you love me."

"I love you, Chance. I do love you."

And then he was there.

With Chance's first bold thrust Brooke was swept away in a tide of sensations that seemed to reach to the very recesses of her soul. Chance slid his arm under her hips to bring her up against him, to fill her. Their bodies moved as one in an ebb and flow, faster, harder, higher and higher, until Brooke slipped beyond reality as spasms of sensual pleasure rocketed through her.

"Chance!" she called, tightly gripping his shoulders.

"Yes, Brooke, yes," he said and joined her in the place to where she had journeyed, shuddering above her and then collapsing with a throaty moan.

He pushed himself up to rest on his arms and kissed her deeply before attempting to speak.

"Did I hurt you?" he asked quietly.

"No. Oh, no, it was wonderful."

"Yes, it was wonderful, you are wonderful, and I love you. Please, Brooke, please don't be sorry this happened. Don't regret any of it. Let it be to you whatever you choose, but don't be sorry."

"I won't be. Not ever. I promise you that, Chance."

He moved away and shifted her to pull back the blankets, then covered them against the chill of the room. After switching off the light, he nestled her close to his side and rested his lips lightly on her forehead. Within a few minutes his steady breathing told Brooke that he was asleep, and she smiled up into the darkness.

A calmness came over her, a peace like she had never known before. She had gone to Chance willingly, totally and joyously. But with that decision an event had taken place of even greater magnitude. It had been neither preplanned nor calculated, but Brooke was the recipient of even more than the wondrous memories of becoming one with Chance. He was her Christmas present and with the end of the holiday would come the heartbreak of goodbye. But unknowingly she had received more, an extension of her gift, one that would be forever cherished.

For with that infinite wisdom given only to woman herself, she knew that Chance had planted his seed deep within her, and she had conceived his child.

Six

———

Brooke woke as the first rays of the winter sun were streaking across the floor. She turned her head to see Chance sleeping next to her and smiled. Her hands slid to rest on her bare, smooth stomach in a warming, protective gesture.

She felt suddenly older, as if she had crossed over an invisible line and at last gained a maturity she had been lacking. She was a woman in love with a man who was unobtainable due to her own inadequacies. She was a woman who would give birth to that man's child. No, she hadn't set out to accomplish this feat, to have this precious life nestled deep within her. But she sensed that this had happened.

And she was filled with joy.

All the love and caring, all the devotion Brooke would have lavished on Chance, she would give to this baby. The trust, bond, would begin from that day and carry them through. The ache in her heart for Chance Tabor would be replaced by the knowledge that she had not really lost him but instead possessed the very essence of his being within her.

Brooke watched Chance sleep, saw the steady rise and fall of his chest, his dark lashes fanned over his tanned cheeks, the shadowy stubble of beard. She loved him with an intensity beyond description. He was her man, her lover, her Santa Claus, her Christmas present. If only the coming together of their bodies had meant a union of their souls. If only she could believe that he was all that he seemed to be. But he was a man, and Brooke did not understand the ways of men.

"I love you, Chance," she whispered.

"I love you, too," he mumbled.

"I didn't mean to wake you."

Chance opened his eyes and turned his head to look at her, a smile on his lips.

"I can't think of a nicer way to start the day," he said, his hand moving to cup her breast. "Good morning, pretty Brooke."

"Good—oh!" she said as he lifted her on top of him.

"Mmmm, you feel great. All soft and warm. I love you," he said, sliding his hand to her nape to lower her lips to his.

As their tongues met, Chance's hands moved down Brooke's back and over the slope of her buttocks. She could feel his arousal beneath her—ready, wanting, heated. She was awash with desire as her breasts were crushed against his chest, and a purring moan escaped her throat. He lifted her upward as though she weighed no more than a feather and drew the rosy bud of one breast into his mouth.

"Oh, Chance," Brooke gasped as her passion heightened.

"I want you so much," he said. "So much."

"Yes!"

Chance's hands moved over her, stroking her as his tongue and teeth gave loving attention to her breasts. Then he grasped her by the waist and lifted her upward. With infinite gentleness he settled her over his thrusting manhood and watched her eyes flutter closed, then open again as the sensations swept through her. She moved against him, filling herself with his maleness, matching his rhythms as he lifted to meet her.

"Oh, Brooke!" he said. "Come with me now, Brooke."

She was so close, so close, struggling, seeking, aching for the illusive treasure and then . . . she was there. In rippling waves of ecstasy, she trembled as the spasms shook her, and she felt Chance shudder beneath her. She went limp and fell forward to be caught against his strong chest and held safely in his arms as they drifted back . . . to now.

"You were incredible," he said, moving her to his side and brushing the moist curls from her forehead.

"I've never felt so wonderful. It was beautiful."

"Think about it, babe. You trusted me to take care of you. You knew I wouldn't hurt you. You did what I was asking of you because you trusted me. Trust enters into all aspects of our lives. If you could give of yourself like you just did, even though it was new, different, simply because you had faith in me, why can't you go further? Why can't you believe that I love you, want to marry you, be with you forever? Why Brooke?"

"I . . ."

"No, don't answer, just think about it. Really think about it, okay?"

"Yes, all right. Oh, I'm sleepy."

"Listen, why don't you sleep and I'll go hit the slopes. Sound good?"

"Perfect. I don't want to move."

"I'll be back in a couple of hours, and we'll have a big breakfast."

"Mmmm."

"Bye, babe—" he chuckled, kissing her on the forehead "—I can tell you're really going to miss me."

"Mmmm."

Brooke was asleep before Chance finished showering and did not hear him leave the room. When she woke an hour later, she stretched leisurely and yawned. As Chance's words filtered through her fogginess, she frowned at the ceiling.

The man had a point, she thought. She had trusted him during their lovemaking, gone to him with no fear or hesitation, with an abandonment that she would not have thought possible. His question was valid. Why couldn't her faith in him go further, encompass more?

"Because I'm frightened, Chance," she said to the empty room. "Scared to death. To believe in you is to believe in my own judgment, and I have a stinky track record." How strange it was to lack confidence in herself in regard to the man she loved and have no doubt in her mind that having his baby was so absolutely right. And it was. She would cherish this child and her memories of Chance.

Brooke showered and dressed, then wandered downstairs to the dining room for a cup of coffee. She decided that she would wait until Chance returned before eating the promised breakfast and, instead, sat by the window and watched the skiers on the distant slopes.

Over an hour later Brooke saw Chance approach. He was dressed in a royal-blue skiing outfit, his cheeks pink from the cold and his thick hair a mass of damp curls. He halted and turned as if someone had called to him, and Brooke could see a man and two women come to where Chance stood. They began to laugh at something that someone had said, and then one of the women stood on tiptoe and kissed Chance full on the mouth. A moment later they waved goodbye, and Chance continued to the hotel.

On trembling legs Brooke walked over to meet him. She felt as though she had been dealt a physical blow as she was unable to erase from her mind the image of the woman kissing Chance with such familiarity. Had he arranged the rendezvous last night when he had taken so long at the bar? Had he known when he had made love to her that he had plans to meet another woman this morning? Now, she supposed, he would waltz in here and intend to kiss her!

"Hey, nice surprise," Chance said when he entered. "Man, the skiing was great. Ready for some food?"

"Fine," Brooke said quietly.

"What's wrong? I'm sorry I was gone so long, but there was a line at the lifts."

"That lipstick really isn't your shade, Chance."

"What? Oh," he said, wiping the back of his hand over his mouth, "orange isn't my color, huh?"

"Was that supposed to be funny?"

"Wait a minute here. I didn't kiss Claudia, she kissed me. In fact, Claudia kisses everyone she knows and some she doesn't. You're really upset, aren't you?"

"No."

"Yes, you are. You looked out that window, saw a woman kissing me and drew your own conclusions. Now I'm explaining what happened and I'm telling you the truth. Claudia is a kisser. It's her trademark or something. I know her, but I've never been out with her. I suppose I could go find her and have her verify what I'm saying, but I'd rather you believed *me*. Well, Brooke?"

"This is ridiculous," Brooke said. "I haven't the foggiest notion whether you're telling the truth. I think I'll believe you because I'm hungry and I'd rather go eat than stand here and argue."

"No, damn it!" Chance roared. "We're not budging until I've been declared innocent!"

"Hey, buddy," a man yelled, "you look guilty as sin to me!"

"No way," a woman said. "He's sexy, not guilty. Or guilty of being sexy. Or... whatever."

"Knock it off!" Chance bellowed. "I have been unjustly accused of a crime I did not commit!"

"Okay!" Brooke shrieked. "I believe you! I do! Just shut up, for Pete's sake!"

"How do I know you really believe me?" Chance said, squinting at her.

"Is my nose growing? No, it is not. Is my stomach growling? Yes, it is. I am now going to go eat. You can join me or go kiss Claudia, whatever strikes your fancy."

"I did not kiss Claudia!"

"I think you need a lawyer, man," a passing waiter said.

"That's all," Brooke said, spinning around and marching away. "I've had it. This is a circus."

"Damn it," Chance said, stalking after her.

Out in the lobby Brooke stopped dead in her tracks, nearly causing Chance to topple over her. She turned around, threw her arms around his neck and kissed him.

"Hi," she said, smiling brightly.

"Hi?"

"Yes, hi. Chance, I sounded like a jealous shrew in there and I'm not. The problem isn't your conduct, it's mine. I'm such a flea brain I can't decipher the truth when I see or hear it. You are my Christmas present, and I want to keep you for the holidays just like we planned. Therefore, you can kiss everyone from here to Chicago and it won't matter because I am going to believe only what I want to. But the funny part is, I suddenly know you didn't kiss Claudia. I just know it."

"You believe me?"

"Yes, I do. Dumb-dumb that I am, I do."

"That's great!" he said, smiling at her. "Terrific! It's a major breakthrough. I told you the truth and you believed me."

"Well..."

"Let's go eat. I'm going to buy you the best breakfast in the place."

In the dining room they ordered their meal, and then Chance said that he was going to dash upstairs and change into dry clothes since his skiing outfit was uncomfortably damp.

Brooke propped her elbows on the table and rested her chin in her hands. She *had* believed Chance. Oh, it felt good. It was dangerous and probably not too bright to trust herself like that, but it created a warm glow within her. Chance had spoken and she had listened, really listened, and the doubt had been swished away.

All that commotion over a kisser named Claudia who wore orange lipstick? That wasn't even the issue. The important thing was that Brooke had looked deep within herself and had known that Chance was not lying to her. Oh, yes, it felt good, like a benevolent cloak wrapping her in comfort. Were there more truths for her to find? Greater faith to build in her judgment regarding this man? Was it possible that... No! She mustn't fall prey to herself. *She* was her own worst enemy. She was the one who dealt the lethal blows to her person by believing in herself when she shouldn't.

"That's better," Chance said, sitting down opposite her again. "Toasty warm, and here comes the food."

They were silent for a few minutes as they consumed the delicious meal.

"Brooke," Chance said finally, "would you like to go on a sleigh ride before we have to catch our plane?"

"Oh, yes, that sounds like fun."

"Okay. I'm very glad you came with me this weekend, Brooke. It's not just because we made love, either. I hope you realize, though, how much that meant to me, how wonderful it was."

"Yes, I feel the same way."

"But more than that has happened. You believed me in what could have been a lousy misunderstanding. It's a beginning, Brooke, and it's important. Listen, when I said I was working late those nights before we came here, did you question it?"

"Well, no, I didn't."

"Don't you see? There's more trust between us than you even realize. I'm not going to press the issue now. I just ask that you think about it. Brooke, I love you so much. I want to marry you and celebrate next Christmas with our first child."

"A...baby?"

"Yes, Brooke. Our baby. Of course, if you didn't want a family right away, we'd wait because having a child is so special, so glorious, that it should be decided together, planned for. It should never be a decision made by only one-half of the people involved."

"It...shouldn't?" Brooke said, a knot tightening in her stomach.

"No, never. In my mind I picture sitting down and talking about it with my wife and then making the most beautiful love imaginable. I want to know where and when my child is conceived so I'm part of his life from the moment he begins. Okay, enough heavy talk. Let's go for a sleigh ride. I'll go up and get our coats."

"Yes, all right." Brooke nodded. Oh, dear heaven, what had happened? She knew, *knew*, she was carrying Chance's baby at that very moment, and he'd had no say in it. No, that wasn't entirely true. She hadn't created this child alone! She and Chance had come together by mutual consent—

giving, taking, sharing. The outcome of that union was theirs to deal with as a couple; it was not her sole responsibility as a single entity.

No, wait, that was crazy. The child was hers because after Christmas she'd no longer have Chance. She'd fallen under his spell for a moment there when he had spoken of having a child they had planned together after they were married. Married? Oh, she loved him, wanted to be his wife, spend the rest of her life with him.

And Chance? The soft, gentle warmth in his eyes when he told of their future together was mesmerizing, rendering her incapable of thinking straight. He appeared so sincere, so loving. Did he really want all those things he spoke so reverently of? Did he want to marry her, forsaking all others, including the Claudias? Was her Santa Claus, her Christmas present, not just a whimsical fantasy? Was Chance Tabor real? She was so confused.

Brooke pushed the turmoil in her mind away and thoroughly enjoyed the ride in the sleigh. A brown horse with a necklace of jingling bells carried them over the snowy ground with a top-hat-clad driver sitting high on a bench holding the reins. Brooke and Chance nestled under a blanket, snuggled close to each other, their cheeks and noses pink from the cold, constant smiles on their faces. It was absolutely marvelous.

In the middle of the afternoon, they had a light lunch and then returned to the room to pack. Chance pulled Brooke into his arms and kissed her so passionately that she was trembling.

"I hate to leave," he said, close to her lips. "This has been so special."

"I know."

"I want to make love to you now, this minute. I wonder if they'd hold the plane for us."

"I somehow doubt it."

"Oh, Brooke," he said, pulling her even more tightly to his chest, "would you say it again? Tell me that you love me?"

"I love you, Chance," she whispered.

"And I love you. Somehow I am going to convince you of that. You are my world, my sunshine. If I had my choice, we would be married right away. We'd celebrate this Christmas as husband and wife and every Christmas after this together. I'm asking you to trust in me, believe in me and marry me. I love you," he said, his voice choked with emotion.

A stillness came over Brooke, an inner peace like none she had ever felt before. She slowly lifted her head, knowing what she would see. There in the sapphire pools of Chance's eyes were tears. He made no attempt to hide them from her as he looked down at her. He was baring his soul, leaving himself open for hurt, pain. He was vulnerable, at the mercy of her words and actions.

Chance Tabor truly loved her.

"Oh, Chance," she said, a sob catching in her throat.

"No, don't say anything. I understand that you're not ready for all this yet, but I had to tell you what's in my heart, my mind. I know you don't believe in my love."

But she did! she thought wildly. She did! She was free of the doubts, the inner turmoil at last. Chance had beaten the insidious ghosts of her past mistakes and errors in judgment and won the victory. He loved her, she loved him, and it was real.

But unintentionally she had betrayed him. She had not set out with a predetermined plan to make love with Chance and conceive his child, but it had happened. Oh, dear heaven, what was she going to do?

"We'd better go," Chance said quietly.

"Yes."

"Hey, don't look so sad. We can come back again if you like."

"That . . . would be nice."

"Are you all right?"

"Yes, Chance, I'm fine. I just want you to know that these hours have meant a great deal to me. I'll cherish every moment. This trip and you are the nicest Christmas presents I've ever had."

"Oh, Brooke," he said, taking possession of her mouth in a searing kiss.

Chance smiled at her gently, warmly, then tugged her curls around her cheeks, ran his fingertips over the nine freckles on her nose and then picked up their suitcases. Brooke forced a smile onto her lips and left the room with an aching heart and tears burning at the back of her eyes.

Somehow Brooke managed to chat pleasantly with Chance during the flight and then the drive to her apartment once they had stepped off the plane in Denver. As they approached her door, she took her key from her purse.

"Uh-oh," Chance said, "there's a message taped to your door. Know any friendly bill collectors?"

"It's from Gran," Brooke said after pulling the paper free. "She wants us to come over as soon as we get here."

"Okay. Let's put your suitcase inside first."

Gran answered the door the moment Brooke knocked.

"Come in," she said, "Hello, Chance. I feel as though I know you."

"Gran, is something wrong?" Brooke asked.

"It's Joey. He's passed out on my bed. He came staggering over here looking for Chance."

"Joey is drunk?" Brooke said. "He doesn't drink. Did he say what's bothering him?"

"I couldn't make much sense out of it," Gran said. "It's something to do with Julie, and Joey needed to talk to his buddy Chance. Poor Joey. He's going to be so sick when he

wakes up. I steered him toward the bed and he's out cold.
He's been here about an hour.''

"Let me see him alone," Chance said, shrugging out of
his jacket. "Maybe you should make some coffee."

"I'll do it right away," Gran said.

Chance disappeared into the bedroom, and Brooke followed Gran into the kitchen.

"I've never known Joey to drink," Brooke said.
"Never."

"He's a very upset young man," Gran said. "How was
your trip?''

"Wonderful, very special."

"There's a glow about you, Brooke. The lovely look of a
woman in love."

"I do love Chance, Gran," Brooke said, hardly above a
whisper.

"And?"

"And what?"

"Are you going to listen to your heart instead of that silly
head of yours and grab some happiness for yourself with
Chance?"

"It's very complicated, Gran. I just can't discuss it right
now, or I'll cry for a year."

"Oh, honey, I wish—"

"Well," Chance said, coming into the kitchen, "the best
laid plans of mice and men. Brooke, you were right and the
rest of us were full of baloney. Everything backfired."

"What do you mean?" Brooke asked.

"It's Julie. She called Joey and said her dream had come
true. She loves every part of that modeling junk, and the
guy in L.A. says she has a terrific career ahead of her. Joey's
been benched. He's out of the ball game."

"Oh, no," Brooke said.

"That foolish girl," Gran said. "I'd like to turn her over
my knee."

"Julie's going to phone you, Brooke," Chance said, "and bring you up to date on her plans. Gran, I'll give some of that coffee to Joey and then I'll take him home with me. I've never seen a guy so blown away. He's really hurting. He loves Julie and he's lost her. Damn, I hate this. Love isn't supposed to rip someone up. I guess Julie has the right to do what she wants, but right now she seems so selfish."

"Sometimes," Gran said, "we make a decision in a breath of a moment that affects the rest of our lives. It's sad what we do to ourselves. I pray that Julie will be happy, but I don't believe for a minute that the choice she made is right for her. She's been caught up in the glitter and excitement, and she's not thinking straight. Beebee, you were the only one who realized Joey had made a mistake, and you claim you have poor judgment. You're wiser than you give yourself credit for."

"Not...really," Brooke said, her hand coming to rest on her flat stomach. "Decisions made in the breath of a moment."

"What?" Chance said.

"Nothing. The coffee is ready," Brooke said as a wave of icy misery swept over her.

A half hour later Chance hauled a muttering Joey out the door. Chance managed to give Brooke a quick kiss, issued a promise to call her later and then disappeared with his tall friend in tow. Brooke felt the sudden need to be alone and quickly told Gran that she was exhausted from the trip to Aspen and in dire need of a nap.

Inside her apartment Brooke flung herself across her bed and cried. She cried for the freedom from her past that she had gained too late, and for the love of Chance Tabor that was real and honest and which she could no longer claim. She cried for the child nestled deep within her that had not been created according to Chance's master plan.

Chance felt that Julie was wrong to have chosen a career over Joey, but Julie had always been honest and straight-forward about her hopes and dreams to become a model. There had been nothing devious or secretive about Julie's actions, Brooke realized. Joey had heard Julie speak of her ambitions, called her bluff and lost. Yet Chance judged Julie as being selfish because Joey was so deeply hurt. Chance was intelligent enough to know that Julie had done nothing wrong but still insisted that Joey's pain was Julie's fault. Julie was innocent of any wrongdoing.

But how would Chance view Brooke?

Would he judge her as he did Julie, pushing aside what he would know on an intellectual level was true? Would sound reasoning prevail and he would recognize and accept his part in the creation of their child? Or would he narrow his eyes and hold fast to his set plan of knowing when his baby was conceived? Would he place the entire blame on Brooke?

She had listened to her heart instead of her mind, gone to Chance willingly, filled with trust and joy. She had lived for the moment of ecstasy that they had shared, giving no thought to the ramifications. And he hadn't thought of the consequences, either.

Yes, oh, yes, she wanted Chance's baby. If only he didn't have such etched-in-stone ideas of how it should come to be. It was suddenly frightening and confusing. In a handful of hours, her life had completely changed.

"Oh, dear," she sniffled, rolling onto her back. And now what? Chance was stubborn when he'd made up his mind about something. He had stated adamantly how his child would come to be. He had thought it through, pro-grammed it into his future, and that was that. Brooke had followed the instincts of her heart at a given moment. They didn't mesh, view things in the same way.

All she could give Chance now was the fulfillment of her promise to be his Christmas present. She would make the numbered days as special for him as possible and rejoice in the sound of his laughter. Maybe, just maybe, some of the memories would sustain him when she walked out of his life on December twenty-sixth. There would be no more Santa Claus, no more Chance.

The ringing of the telephone brought Brooke wearily to her feet and into the living room where she answered the summons with a subdued greeting.

"Beebee?"

"Julie, how are you?"

"I'm fine. Have you seen Joey?"

"Yes, and he's pretty upset."

"I know. Oh, Beebee, I feel as though I'm being torn in two. I love my Joey, but I want this career so badly. It's like something burning inside me. I'd come to resent Joey if I threw it all away for him. He doesn't understand and I guess I can't blame him."

"What exactly are your plans?"

"I'll call work tomorrow and quit my job. I've got some modeling assignments already. I'll stay over here through the holidays, see my family, then come back to collect the rest of my things. That will give you time to decide if you want another roommate or to move to a smaller place. I'm leaving you in a bind, too."

"No, you're not. I'll be fine. Julie, are you very sure you want to do this?"

"Yes, Beebee, I've made up my mind. I never intended to hurt Joey. I love him and I would have been proud to be his wife but not now, not yet. His dream is to have a wife and family, and I'm not ready for that."

"No, of course not. A baby...should be planned, wanted by both people. I understand what you're saying, I really do."

"Thank you, Beebee. I'm feeling so guilty about Joey and I miss him and you. How's Chance?"

"He's fine, wonderful. We had a super time in Aspen."

"And? Does he get to hang around longer than the rest of the Santas in the world?"

"No, Julie. I'm only seeing Chance through Christmas."

"Oh, Beebee, can't you trust and believe in him even a little?"

"There's so much more to it than that. I'll explain when you come back for your things. In the meantime, please take care of yourself and be happy."

"I will. Be kind to my Joey, Beebee. He's so very special, and he needs a friend."

"He's with Chance right now."

"Good. I love you, kiddo. Ta-ta for a while."

"Bye, Julie."

Brooke replaced the receiver and sank onto the sofa, pressing her fingertips to her temples. She was going to miss Julie terribly. They had been like sisters, sharing the joys and sorrows of their lives. Changes. So many, many changes.

Brooke ate a dinner of soup and salad and then unpacked her suitcase. She turned the television on, then off, then on again, only to press the switch and quiet the chatter one last time. The book that she attempted to read held no interest, and she ended up straightening the kitchen cupboards in restless, nervous energy. When a knock sounded at the door at eight, she flung it open with the intention of talking for an hour to whomever it might be, encyclopedia salesman included.

"Chance!"

"Hi, babe," he said, coming into the room. "I brought Joey back to get his car and thought I'd pop in. Okay?"

"More than okay. Take off your coat. Want some coffee? A sandwich? Have you had dinner? I could fix—"

"Hush, motor mouth," he said, pulling her into his arms and kissing her deeply.

"I guess I was babbling a bit," she said breathlessly when he released her. "How's Joey?"

"Sober, nursing a hangover and a broken heart. Man, I just spent hours with that guy and heard him go on and on about his love for Julie. Does she have any idea what she's thrown away?"

"That's not really fair, Chance. Julie has the right to make choices for herself. She loves Joey, but she also wants a career."

"Oh, yeah, right. People always slice the person they love into a million pieces."

"She didn't intend to hurt him."

"Well, she sure as hell did. She's only thinking of herself, her own needs. Joey is a human being with feelings, too. I told him to forget her, just start patching himself back together and move on."

"But, Chance, Julie might change her mind!"

"So? A man has some pride, Brooke. What's Joey supposed to do? Hang around like a whipped puppy hoping for a pat on the head? Nope. No way. The guy had a dream. Joey wanted a wife, a baby. From where I'm sitting, that isn't too much to ask."

"I . . . Would you like some coffee?"

"What? Oh, yeah, thanks."

"I'll be right back. Make yourself comfortable."

In the kitchen Brooke drew a steadying breath before attempting to prepare the coffee. Chance's words hammered at her mind, screamed their message over and over. A man had his pride, could not be shattered by the woman he loved and be expected to hang around for more. Joey's dream of a wife and child was Chance's as well. But Chance went further in his mental scenario. He wanted to plan the conception of his baby, know the time and place it had occurred and rejoice in the knowledge. Julie, Chance felt, deserved no second opportunity at a life with Joey Rather. Chance granted no quarter and stood firm in his beliefs. Brooke knew that Chance would never accept what had happened in Aspen.

"Coffee," she said, forcing a lightness into her voice as she reentered the living room.

"Smells good. Did you speak to Julie?"

"Yes, she called," Brooke said, sitting down next to him on the sofa. "Let's not discuss it anymore, okay?"

"Well, I just wondered what you were going to do about this apartment."

"The rent is paid until the end of the month. I'll decide then when Julie comes for her things."

"I see. This would be a great opportunity for me to propose again, but I'll restrain myself. If I say it too often, you'll probably tell me to put a cork in it."

"Drink your coffee," she smiled.

"Your Gran is a nice lady. She'd be perfect for my grandfather."

"Are you playing cupid?"

"Hey, if I had it my way, the whole world would be in love. It's a nice place to be."

"Would you like to watch television?"

"Sure. What's on?"

"Chance, would you spend the night with me?"

"I beg your pardon?"

"Oh, dear, that was rather brash, wasn't it?"

"It was wonderful, but I can't quite believe you said it. Are you serious?"

"Yes, I am."

"Why?"

"Because it's been such a lovely weekend and we could make it last that much longer."

"Sold. I'll stay. You are full of surprises, Brooke."

"Aren't I though?" she said under her breath.

"Guess what? I left my shaving kit in the hotel in Aspen. Dumb, huh?"

"You're one of those absentminded geniuses," Brooke said with a laugh.

"I am? Hey, that sounds classy. I like it. You know, you could rent out Julie's room to a Saint Bernard. Just make sure he has a good, steady job."

Brooke smiled and snuggled closer to Chance's side. They settled on a spy movie and talked in hushed tones giving their opinion about who had done it.

Brooke shook her head in wonder at her bold request of asking Chance to spend the night, but she wanted, needed, him there close to her. Their hours together were being counted down, checked off, were ticking away. Each must be savored, cherished, treasured. Each was a part of her Christmas gift.

"It was starting to snow when I drove over," Chance said. "Denver is turning into a Christmas card again. What a great time of year."

"Yes, it certainly is."

"A lot has changed since we met, huh?"

"Yes."

"And it's good. It's good, Brooke. I love you so much. I have to say it within a set time frame, or I'll break out in hives. I love you. Quit tugging on your curls. My loving you is nothing to get shook about. It's just an honest-to-goodness fact. I think that Italian guy is the crook."

"What? Oh, no, he isn't. It's the bald Greek."

"Too obvious."

"Wanna bet?"

"Oh, you're asking for it. Okay, Bradley, I'll wager the cooking of breakfast tomorrow morning."

"You're on, Tabor."

"I'll give you my menu later. I want the works."

"Shhh. I don't want to miss any clues that will point the finger at my Greek."

"It's the Italian."

"Shhh!"

The crook turned out to be a ninety-pound grandmotherly type with blue hair who shot poison darts from a cane she used to help her walk. Chance ranted and raved, booed and hissed and declared the movie a flop. Brooke dissolved in a fit of laughter that was silenced by Chance's lengthy kiss. They agreed to fix breakfast together the next morning.

Their lovemaking in Brooke's bed was slow and sweet and sensuous. They touched, kissed, stroked the other until passions flared into raging flames and they could hold back no longer. In a glorious celebration, in perfect synchrony, in harmony and bliss, they exploded upon their private shore.

They slept at last with their heads resting on the same pillow and hands entwined. It was the slumber of lovers—sated, spent, contented. When they woke at dawn, they reached once again for each other and journeyed to their treasured place.

"Food. I'm starving," Chance said finally, swinging off the bed and peering through the drapes covering the window. "Holy cow!"

"What's wrong?" Brooke said sleepily.

"We'd better turn on the radio, my sweet. It's a giant marshmallow out there. I have a feeling we're snowed in."

"Really?" Brooke said, hurrying to look at the scene outside. "My goodness, it's really howling and the snow is falling so thickly I can't see across the street. Brrr. It's cold in here. Funny, I didn't notice that earlier."

"I'll push up the thermostat." Chance chuckled. "Body heat is much more effective, however."

"I'm turning blue," Brooke said, diving back into bed.

Chance tugged on his jeans and went into the living room, only to retrace his steps a few minutes later and pick up Brooke's clock off the nightstand.

"Windup job. No wonder it's working," he said. "There's no heat, electricity, phone, nothing."

"We're pioneers on the frontier!" Brooke yelled, pulling the blankets up to her chin.

"Damn," Chance said, sitting down on the edge of the bed and reaching for his shoes. "No heat. I've got to get to my office."

"What? Why? Chance, you can't go out in this."

"I have to. I have very delicate computer equipment down there that is highly susceptible to extreme heat or cold. I have one room set up with battery-operated heaters. I've got to move everything."

"I'll go with you."

"No. It's wicked out there. You stay put. I have enough to worry about already."

"But I want to go with you."

"I said no, Brooke," he said sharply, grabbing his shirt and striding from the room.

Brooke untangled herself from the blankets and scrambled off the bed and into the living room. She arrived just in time to see Chance closing the front door behind him as he left the apartment.

Seven

By two o'clock that afternoon Brooke would have killed for a hot fudge sundae.

She was a nervous wreck.

The wind and snow continued to howl outside, and the apartment was cold, dark and lonely. Gran had knocked on the door in midmorning to announce that she was going down to the second floor to play gin rummy by candlelight with a group of ladies from the building.

Brooke had dug out the fancy candlesticks and candles but had decided not to light them since she had no idea how long the blackout would last and she could at least still see in the dreary luminescence. Denver was apparently buried in snow, but with no radio or television to keep her informed, Brooke could only guess at the intensity of the storm.

And Chance, her Chance, was out in it somewhere.

Brooke had dressed and then stared out the bedroom window at the blizzard for an undetermined length of time. A knot of fear had tightened in her stomach as she envisioned Chance attempting to drive in the inclement weather. She was unable to clearly see the street below to know if the traffic was even moving.

Giving up her vigil, she had wandered through the apartment, straightening, dusting and periodically adding another sweater to her already bulky attire. By noon she was so angry at Chance that she was sputtering. How dare he go charging off to attend to computers and floppy disks or whatever and leave her to worry and stew, and to freeze to death on top of it! But then the anger had dissipated, and she was once more frantic with concern. She had eaten an orange, a handful of cookies and a tomato. Her stomach hurt. Her head hurt. She wanted, needed, a hot fudge sundae.

During the course of the day, Brooke had intermittently switched on lights to see if they might be working and soon had lost track of which ones were on and which were off. Not that it mattered. The apartment was a dark, gloomy, cold cave, and she was going out of her mind. The storm raged on and on.

And Chance was out in it somewhere.

She was going to strangle him!

No, she was going to fling herself into his arms when he returned.

That is, if she didn't shoot him first. But, oh, dear heaven, where was he? And why didn't he come walking through that door?

At three o'clock Brooke ate a carrot, took an aspirin and flopped onto the sofa in a dejected heap.

"Aaak!" she screamed as the room suddenly came alive with bright lights from the lamps and the television flickered into focus. There was a clinking, clunking, pinging noise as the heat rattled up through the vents and spewed its warmth into the room.

"Thank goodness," Brooke sighed, getting to her feet to adjust the television and welcome a human voice.

"... worst storm in decades," the announcer was saying. "Electricity is gradually being restored through the brave efforts of the crews working under these adverse conditions. Everyone is asked to stay in their homes as visibility is poor and driving nearly impossible. There is no sign of a letup, and the weather service reports a new storm front has moved in. Denver is at a standstill. I repeat, stay in your homes. We will continue to bring you updated reports from this channel."

"Hear that, Tabor? You were supposed to stay put," Brooke said, marching to the kitchen to make a cup of tea.

By four o'clock Brooke had peeled off her extra clothes to a normal layer of jeans and a sweatshirt, the apartment was toasty warm and glowing with light and the television announcer droned on about the blizzard. The telephone was still out of order, and Chance had not returned.

A knock at the door brought Brooke running to answer it. She flung it open and then simply stared at the creature before her. It was covered in snow and crusty ice, and it was shaking from head to foot.

"Chance?" she whispered. "Chance, is that you?"

"Yes ... it's ... me."

"Come in," she said, grabbing him by his jacket and hauling him into the room.

"Ohhh," he moaned. "I'm frozen. Frozen!"

"Take off your clothes. No, wait. I'll start the shower first. No! Maybe I should give you tea or ... I know! Brandy. Yes, that's it. A good stiff drink to—"

"Brooke, I could die while you're making up your mind. Run me a tubful of hot water, okay?"

"Yes, right now," she said, running into the bathroom.

Chance followed slowly behind, moving like a stiff robot whose joints needed oiling.

"Help me out of my clothes," he said in the bathroom. "Ohhh, I have never been so cold. Never!"

Brooke tugged and pulled, huffed and puffed and even swore a few times as she removed the soggy clothes from Chance's body. He moved carefully into the tub and pulled up his knees so that he could fit, letting out a deep sigh after dunking his head and popping back up above the surface. Brooke knelt on the floor and looked at him anxiously.

"I've been so worried about you," she said. "What happened?"

"I got to the office all right, took care of the equipment and started back. Man, what a mess. I couldn't drive in that stuff and there're no buses, taxis, nothing. I plowed through on foot."

"You walked? Oh, Chance."

"I couldn't call to tell you I was going to hole up somewhere, and I figured you'd be pretty upset if I didn't show up so I kept pushing."

"I don't know what to say. That was so wonderful of you to be concerned about me. It was borderline dumb, but . . . dear and sweet. Thank you."

"Want to crawl in this tub with me?" he grinned.

"*You* hardly fit. You don't need any company. I'm going to fix you something hot to drink. Are you hungry?"

"Starved."

"Okay, I'll whip us up some dinner. As soon as you're warmed through, go crawl into bed. You're a little short on dry clothes. Chance, I mean it. What you did, walking all the way back here, was so special."

"I love you, Brooke. I didn't want to do anything to upset you. I knew what I had to do. It wasn't even complicated."

Brooke leaned over and kissed Chance full on the mouth before pushing herself to her feet and heading for the kitchen. Her heart was nearly overflowing with love for him. To him, the trek through the snow was a simple case of something he had to do. To her, it was a lovely message of caring.

She loved him so very much, needed, wanted him in her days and nights for the remainder of her life. His love was the most beautiful gift that she had ever received, and she did not want to have to give it back the day after Christmas.

Maybe... she wasn't pregnant. Maybe... No, she was carrying Chance's child. She knew it. She just... knew it. But maybe he'd understand that she hadn't actually set out to conceive his baby. And he had, after all, been the other half of what had taken place. Yes, of course! Chance would understand. No, Chance would *not* understand, and she was kidding herself if she figured that he would. He had very set ideas on the subject of his future children, and she had not followed the proper plan.

She wanted Chance's baby, had niggling fears but no regrets that it was nestled within her. But, oh heavens, she wanted its father, too. Oh, great. Now she was feeling sorry for herself!

"Knock it off, Brooke," she told herself firmly as she set the dishes on the tray.

Chance was burrowed under the blankets on her bed when Brooke entered the bedroom.

"Rise and shine," she said. "Soup's on."

"I'm cold."

"I don't have anything even close to fitting you. Oh, wait. I think there's a sweatshirt of Joey's in Julie's room. Turn around and take this tray."

"Too cold."

"Good grief," she said, setting it on the dresser and marching out of the room.

Joey's sweatshirt was enormous, and Chance agreed to emerge from under the blankets to put it on.

"The top half of me is warm," he said. "What about the rest of me?"

"We'll think of something. Here, let's eat."

They sat propped against the pillows and consumed the food, Chance declaring that he would probably live after all.

"I would not have made a good pioneer," he said, setting the tray on the floor. "I'm not into roughing it. I wonder if my car will ever defrost. Did you have a lousy day?"

"Yep. Julie's the smart one. She's out in California where it's warm and sunny."

"Let's not discuss Julie, Brooke. I know you two are very close, and I don't want to get in an argument about what she's done to Joey. I don't think we see it from the same point of view."

"Probably not. I don't presume to be able to think like a man. That's an impossible task."

"Well, all I have to say is that I don't feel Julie really loves Joey. If she did, she wouldn't have hurt him like that. There is such a thing as compromise, you know."

"Chance, Joey didn't offer to compromise."

"He never had a chance to."

"Oh? Are you saying he'd have agreed to marry Julie, have her pursue her career in modeling and waited to have a family?"

"Well, maybe not. He was pretty firm on what he wanted. But then so am I. I want to marry Brooke Bradley, go on a lovely honeymoon definitely to someplace warm, set up our home together and then agree on when to have a baby."

"I see," Brooke said quietly. "With no room for compromise?"

"Well, sure. Size of wedding, where to live, when to start a family—all that stuff is up for negotiation. I'm easy to get along with."

"But the order of events?"

"They're logical." He shrugged. "Honeymoons come after weddings, you know."

"Some people live together in this day and age."

"True, but that's not my thing. I want to be married, Brooke."

"And know when your child is conceived," she said, hardly above a whisper.

"Oh, yes," he said, lacing his fingers behind his head. "What a moment in my life that will be. Think about it, Brooke. You and I would be creating a miracle together. When we make love now, it's an incredibly beautiful experience. Then, on that special night, we'd come to each other and a new life would begin inside of you because of our love for each other. The thought of it blows my mind. I would treasure it forever in my heart, my very soul."

Brooke couldn't speak as her throat tightened with unshed tears.

"I sure wish you'd marry me," Chance said in a hushed voice. "I really, really do."

"I can't."

"We'll see. Joey may be benched, but the whistle hasn't blown on my ball game yet. Come here, my Christmas present. I thought you were going to suggest a way to warm up the part of me not covered by this sweatshirt. Hey, is something wrong? You look like you're about to cry."

"No. No, I'm fine. It's just been a long day, and I was worried about you. Please, Chance, make love to me. Now, right now. I don't want to talk or think, just make love to me."

"My pleasure, Brooke." He smiled, pulling her close. "The night is ours."

And it was.

The raging blizzard and the long, tedious day were forgotten. There was only the splendor of their union, the celebration of becoming one and soaring above time and space. Brooke woke in the night and reached for Chance, caressing and kissing him until he moved over her with a powerful thrust of his manhood. Tears spilled onto her cheeks, and she held him to her breasts as if never again to let him go. When he looked at her questioningly, she smiled to relieve his concern and soon he slept, leaving Brooke to stare into the darkness.

The snow stopped sometime during the night, and the road crews were out in force at dawn to clear the streets for the brave souls who would attempt to go to work. The telephone was miraculously restored to working order, and it rang as Brooke shuffled toward the kitchen to make coffee. Her boss greeted her cheerfully and told her to take the day off since he had no intention of budging from in front of his fireplace. He said that he would see her the next day.

"No can do," Chance said when Brooke suggested that they spend a lazy day together. "My people will be in and we're behind schedule. I'll probably have to work late tonight. I hope the buses are running. I've got to get downtown."

"You can use my car."

"No, you may decide to go out before you get cabin fever. Oh, man, cancel the bus. I've got to get a taxi so I can go home and get some fresh clothes. I'd better hustle."

"You don't want breakfast?"

"No time," he said, heading for the shower. "Duty calls."

Chance's clothes were dry but stiff, and he was grumbling under his breath as he pulled them on.

"Have to get those machines moved back," Chance muttered as he headed toward the door.

"Hey, aren't you going to kiss me goodbye?"

"Oh, yeah, sure," he said, retracing his steps and giving her a peck. "I'll call you later. The power had better stay steady today. Did you know that power dips can wipe out an entire program? See ya."

Brooke opened her mouth, shut it and smiled as the door closed on Chance's back. Her absentminded computer genius was absolutely marvelous.

She had a choice, Brooke decided, as she sank into a bubble bath. She could sit around all day and completely depress herself over her precarious relationship with Chance Tabor or get out of the apartment and think about something else. She was definitely going out. She'd wait until everyone was safely to work before tackling the slushy streets and then venture forth for some fresh air.

After dressing in jeans and a sweater, Brooke pulled a box from the hall closet that contained the Christmas decorations that she and Julie had collected over the past years. The two women had always put up a small tree and exchanged gifts before Julie left for California to be with her family. Brooke traditionally saw Gran on Christmas morning and spent a quiet day with her father.

But this year? she thought as she hung two stockings on the closet door. No Julie, no father, no Gran, no...Chance? He had a mother, father, grandfather and oodles of other relatives for all she knew. He would, of course, spend the day with them, and she did not presume to intrude on a family. She'd be alone. Well, there was nothing she could do about it. And next year? She would sit by her Christmas tree with Chance's baby in her arms, but still there would be no Chance.

It had been only a handful of days since Brooke had stood in line to sit on Santa Claus's lap to pay her debt to Julie. So many lives had changed since then. So many. And a new life had begun deep within her, would grow as her body nurtured it and then be born healthy and strong. In spite of the doubts that Brooke harbored regarding her ability to know truth when faced with it, of these facts she was sure. She just . . . knew.

A wreath was on the apartment door, a silver bell hanging from the kitchen light, a green-and-red garland twisted across the top of the sofa and clusters of holly on the end tables. The tree lights were in working order and the small supply of ornaments all checked for hooks. Determined not to be gloomy, Brooke hummed as she worked and nodded in satisfaction when her chores were completed. She grabbed her coat and purse and headed out the door.

Brooke drove to the mall where she had met Chance and ate a huge lunch in a cozy restaurant that had wandering carolers serenading the patrons. She then strolled through the mall and allowed herself to be caught up in the festive mood. Her travels brought her to the area where Santa received the children, and she watched as the red-suited man rose from his chair and put a sign up that said Time to Feed the Reindeer.

As the Santa approached her, Brooke squinted at him, trying to see past the cotton beard and eyebrows for any clue that this man might be Chance's grandfather.

"Ho ho ho," The tall man said and then winked at her.

Winked at her with a sapphire blue eye.

"Mr. Tabor?" she said cautiously.

"Ho ho yep. Who wants to know, sweetheart?"

"I'm a friend of Chance's."

"Then you pick your friends well because my grandson is a fine boy. Takes after me. His parents are stuffed shirts. Say, now, you're a pretty little thing. Hold it. Hold it," he said, leaning toward her. "Don't move."

"What?" Brooke said, her eyes wide.

"Nine. Nine freckles on your nose. You're Brooke."

"Oh, good heavens," she said, blushing.

"Come on, honey, you can watch me eat my peanut but-
ter sandwich, and we'll talk about our favorite person.
Chance."

Brooke was suddenly being propelled through the crowds
and inside a door marked Employees Only. This man, she
decided ruefully, was definitely related to Chance. He
zoomed around and did whatever felt right.

"Sit," Mr. Tabor said, indicating a chair in a small
dressing room. "These whiskers are hot."

Without the beard Mr. Tabor and Chance strongly re-
sembled each other. They both had the same rugged features and sparkling blue eyes. His face was wrinkled, but his
voice was strong and sounded remarkably like Chance's.
Brooke knew that she was smiling at him and made no attempt to hide it.

"Yes, you are pretty." Mr. Tabor nodded. "Want to
share my sandwich?"

"No, thanks, I just ate."

"So!" he said, taking a big bite. "What are you plan-
ning to do with my grandson?"

"Do?"

"Yeah, do. Smash his heart into a millions pieces? Marry
him? What?"

"Mr. Tabor, I..."

"Call me Willie. I love that name. My son throws a fit
because I refuse to use William and be dignified. How I ever
fathered such a fuddy-duddy I'll never know, but Chance
makes up for it. Well? Do you love my Chance?"

"Yes, Willie, but it's all very complicated."

"Honey, love is always complicated because it's a very
intense emotion. When I married Chance's grandmother,
rest her soul, I was the happiest man on earth. When he
speaks of you, I see in Chance's eyes now what used to be
in mine. Chance has waited a long time for you, Brooke.
Don't hurt him, honey. You're not going to, are you?"

"Yes," she whispered, tears filling her eyes. "Yes, I am, because I have no choice anymore. I didn't intend for this to happen, but it did. I'm sure Chance won't understand because he's already made up his mind as to how it should be. Oh, what a mess!"

"It sounds like it," Willie said, nodding.

"Willie, please know I do love Chance and I never set out to hurt him. He's mine until Christmas and then it's over."

"Here," he said, handing her a tissue. "Blow your nose. Actually, none of this makes any sense at all."

"No, I know it doesn't."

"Chance doesn't realize you did whatever it is you did? This is the craziest conversation I've ever had."

"No, he doesn't have any idea."

"So tell him."

"No!"

"Honey, give the boy an opportunity to judge things for himself."

"He's told me how he feels about it. Oh, it's hopeless. Willie, please don't say anything about this to Chance. Let us have our Christmas, please?"

"Yeah, okay," he sighed. "Then I'll stand around with a dustpan and broom and sweep up the pieces of Chance's heart."

"Thanks, I needed that," Brooke muttered.

"Sorry, honey. I can tell you're ripped up about this, too. There has to be a way to fix whatever it is that's bothering you. It can't be all that bad."

"It is, believe me," she said miserably.

"Do you have a drinking problem?" Willie frowned.

"No." Brooke laughed. "I'm admittedly babbling, though."

"Oh, Brooke, don't throw love away so easily. I lost the woman I loved to death, and there's never been another one like her. Chance, you, your whole future is at stake. Honey, trust my boy to love you with his whole heart, his soul, his mind and body. Chance knows how to forgive. Hell, he forgave me for sticking him with his pin-striped father. Your lives and those of your children are on the line here."

"Our...children?" she said, swallowing heavily.

"Babies? Kids? Those things you have to housebreak? You want to have Chance's baby, don't you?"

"Yes," she said softly, "I want this—his baby."

Willie Tabor pushed himself to his feet and paced the floor for several minutes before sitting back down and readjusting his more than amply padded stomach.

"You're pregnant," he said firmly. "It all fits together now. Every bit of it."

"I never said—"

"Yes, you did. Data," he said, tapping his temple. "I computed it. The whatever that happened is the conception of Chance's child, and I know what that means to him because we've talked about it. That's your secret. Are you sure you're pregnant? You only met Chance a short... Forget that, you're sure. My wife knew with some kind of female instinct, too. Honey, this is a problem."

"Believe me, I know that."

"You'll have to tell him. A man has the right to know his own child. But, Brooke, I don't think Chance is going to take this very well. His feelings on this are so strong. This is not a wonderful situation."

Brooke looked up into the face of Willie Tabor and saw the firm set to the old man's jaw. But in the depths of his blue eyes there was a gentleness, a warmth, an understanding. She nodded her head and fought back her tears before getting slowly to her feet.

"After Christmas," she said, hardly above a whisper. "I'll tell him then. Please let us have our Christmas presents, each other, Willie."

"Of course, honey."

"Thank you for everything. I know now why Chance loves you so much."

"And I know why he loves you. You're a fine girl, sweetheart. You're everything I hoped for for my boy."

"Goodbye, Willie."

Brooke left the rear area and, without really knowing where she was going, ended up in the ice-cream parlor, where she consumed two hot fudge sundaes. Unable to face her empty apartment, she wandered in and out of the stores, not really seeing any of the displays of enticing gifts.

There was a clamor of voices in her head, and Willie Tabor's words pounded against her temples. Willie was sharp and observant, just like Chance. He had pieced together the fragments of Brooke's disjointed statements and computed, as he put it, the correct reason for her turmoil. If Willie could do it, so could Chance, and Brooke would have to be very careful in the days until Christmas. Nothing, nothing, would spoil their holiday.

And Willie was wise. He knew of the importance that Chance placed on the treasured, fleeting second when two came together as one and created a new life, a life that they had planned, formed in a celebration of love and ecstasy.

Brooke stopped in front of a counter and stared at a selection of delicate china figurines. With trembling fingers she cradled one in the palm of her hand. About four inches high, it was a Santa Claus in a red suit, one hand resting on his round tummy, the other placing a finger by the side of his nose. The Santa was smiling with a mischievous expression on his face and looked real enough to say, "Ho ho ho."

It was the perfect gift for Chance, her Santa Claus, and Brooke left the store minutes later with a small box wrapped in gold paper with a matching bow.

After returning to the apartment, Brooke wrapped Julie's present for mailing and spent the next hour in line at the post office sending it on its way to Julie's parents' home in

California. When she stepped off the elevator on her floor in the building once again, she jumped in surprise as a voice boomed down the hallway.

"Ho ho ho!"

"Chance!" she said, hurrying toward him and then stopping abruptly. "A Christmas tree!"

"Absolutely," he said with a grin. "Isn't it a beauty? Smells great, too."

"But I thought you had to work late."

"I delegated authority. Privilege of my rank, plus I worked my little heart out to finish what I was doing. Want to set this up out here, or shall we take it inside?"

"Oh, yes, of course," she said, reaching for her keys.

"Been out and about?"

"I mailed Julie's present to her parents' house. Come in. You're right, that tree smells heavenly."

It was fun. They tuned the radio to a station playing Christmas carols and transformed the tree into a spectacle of twinkling lights and glittering ornaments. They argued over whether the big ones should be hung near the bottom or top of the tree and, with hands entwined, placed the angel in its special place.

And then in the glow of the rainbow colors, Chance pulled her to him and they made sweet, sensuous love in the fairyland world that they had created together.

"Thank you for the tree," Brooke said as he covered her with his sweater.

"Our tree. The first of a million to come. Brooke, we need to discuss Christmas Day. You have Gran and your father and I'm expected at my parents, but I want to be with you."

"Gran is going to Aspen with a group of senior citizens."

"And your father?"

"He's not coming home. He accepted another assignment instead."

"Nice guy," Chance growled. "He didn't care that he wouldn't see you at Christmas?"

"He said we'd celebrate later because it wasn't as though I still believed in Santa Claus."

"Oh, but you do. I'm your Santa Claus, right?"

"Right," she said, smiling.

"Well, the problem is solved. You'll come with me."

"Chance, no. I can't intrude on a family gathering."

"Hey, I love you, remember? Besides, you're my Christmas present and I get to show you off. We won't stay too long after dinner because I make my parents very uptight."

"Will your grandfather be there?"

"Just to eat. He makes them nervous, too. You'll like him, he's a great old guy."

"I'm ... sure I will."

"Then you'll come?"

"I want to be with you."

"Good. This is a very romantic setting we have here, my sweet, but I am so hungry."

"Back to reality." Brooke laughed, reaching for her clothes.

"Brooke?"

"Yes?"

"I love you, babe. I'll always remember putting up our first tree together."

"I love you, too, Chance. It's a beautiful tree."

"We're a great team, partners, halves of a whole."

"I'll make dinner."

It was a lazy, comfortable evening. They ate, cleaned the kitchen together and then watched a Christmas special on television. Brooke groaned when Chance insisted on singing along very loudly and terribly off-key with the choir, and she told him to stick with his computers and not pursue a

career in show business. Later they made love again, and
sometime in the night Chance kissed her deeply, dressed and
left the apartment with the promise to see her the next evening.

The days passed quickly. Brooke was busy at work as her
boss wanted everything caught up before the holidays and
the extra days off. Brooke hurried home each night to prepare dinner for Chance, though he often called her in the
afternoon to say that he was taking her out to eat. They at-
tended a live performance of *A Christmas Carol* and built
another snowman in the park.

The picture of Brooke sitting on Chance's lap when he
was Santa Claus arrived in the mail, and they laughed in
delight at the embarrassed expression on Brooke's face.
Chance bought a frame, and the picture was given a place
of honor on the coffee table.

It was a joyous time, a sharing time, a loving time.
Brooke pushed aside all the distressing thoughts of the future and basked in Chance's love. She was living in a fantasy, she knew it, and she didn't care. These days and nights
were theirs. She wrapped each moment in rosy bliss and
tucked it away as a delicate, loving memory in a special place
in her heart, mind, her very soul.

Gran invited Brooke, Chance and Joey for dinner, and
Gran sniffled her way through opening her presents from
her adopted family. Brooke had signed both hers and
Chance's name to her card, and she hugged him tightly
when he produced his own gift for Gran—lavender scented
soap. Joey was subdued but made every effort to be cheerful. No one mentioned Julie's name.

And the hours continued to tick away.

Just after dinner on Christmas Eve, Julie called to wish
Brooke and Chance a happy holiday. Julie chattered exu-
berantly about her exciting new career and said she would

telephone again with the exact date when she would be returning to collect her belongings.

"Did she even ask about Joey?" Chance inquired after Brooke had replaced the receiver.

"No."

"Incredible." He frowned, shaking his head. "She is one cold lady."

"Let's not get started on that subject."

"You're right. Come sit by me and look at our tree. Man, there are kids who won't sleep tonight all over the country. Ol' Santa is on his way."

"And you, little boy?"

"I'm hiding behind the sofa so I can see him. I'm glad we got organized and had me bring my clothes so we'll be together tomorrow morning. I even remembered my shaving kit. It will also be nice to make love to you and spend the entire night. This thief-in-the-dark routine is getting old."

"You could have stayed over other times, Chance."

"No, Brooke. It would be too easy to fall into a lazy habit of doing that and suddenly more of my stuff is here and bingo! We're living together. No, I want to marry you, live under the same roof as husband and wife."

"No heavy discussions tonight, Chance, okay? We're supposed to be listening for the sound of reindeer's hooves on the roof."

"'Tis true. You listen. I'm having some more of those cinnamon cookies Gran made."

"Keep it up, Tabor, You won't need any padding to play Santa next year."

"I'll just have to get plenty of exercise," he said, wiggling his eyebrows at her. "Indoor activities, you understand."

Late that night Brooke opened her eyes, suddenly wide awake. She felt as though someone had shook her to bring her from her deep slumber, but Chance was sleeping soundly next to her.

She glanced at the clock and knew the summons had been an inner voice. It was midnight. In exactly twenty-four hours Christmas would be over. With the ending of the special day would come the moment of truth. She could delay no longer telling Chance that she carried his child. Brooke would release her hold on her Christmas present.

Eight

Brooke, wake up," Chance said. "It's Christmas!"

"Ohhh, Chance," she moaned, looking at the clock. "It's only six-thirty."

"Up! Up! I'll go make coffee and plug in the tree. Hurry," he said, pulling on jeans and a sweater.

"I swear that man is four years old," Brooke said, reaching for her robe.

After splashing water on her face and brushing her teeth, Brooke decided that she was awake after all and headed for the living room where she stopped dead in her tracks at the sight of what awaited her.

It was the biggest present that she had ever seen and was wrapped in blue paper with snowflakes on it. It was as tall as she was, wider than her outstretched arms and had a lumpy, nondescript shape.

"Interesting, huh?" Chance smiled, coming into the room with two mugs of coffee.

"What is that?"

"Your present, but you can't open it yet."

"Why not?"

"First things first. Come sit by the tree."

Settled on the floor, Chance handed her another gift.

"Wait a minute," Brooke said. "How did that monstrous thing get in here?"

"Santa Claus."

"Chance!"

"Actually, I had it stashed at Gran's and she left her key with me. I snuck over there about five this morning. You're lucky I wasn't a burglar. You never heard a thing. Open that one first."

"Oh, for heaven's sake." Brooke laughed as she tore the paper away. "A gallon jug of hot fudge sauce."

"For emergency situations. It will head off your stress attacks."

"You're crazy."

"Yep."

"Well, this is on about the same par," she said, handing him a flat box.

"Awright," he said, tugging off the lid. "Sweat socks."

"To replace the ones I borrowed that day we made the snowman. I'm keeping that pair. This is for you, too, Chance," she said, giving him the gold foil box.

As Chance unveiled the china Santa, a gentle smile formed on his lips and he kissed Brooke deeply.

"It's perfect," he said. "I'll treasure it always. Thank you, Brooke."

"You're welcome. The minute I saw it I knew it was what I wanted to give you. Now can I open that mountain? I can't stand it another minute."

"Go to it, kid."

It was a Saint Bernard.

It was the biggest, funniest stuffed toy that Brooke had ever seen. It was a Saint Bernard, all right, complete with a whiskey cask under his chin, huge floppy ears and a lop-sided smile. Brooke squealed in delight and threw her arms around Chance's neck.

"He's beautiful," she said, laughing. "Oh, you're so crazy and wonderful."

"Santa always fulfills his promises." Chance grinned. "You asked for a Saint Bernard so you got one."

"The biggest in the world. Where am I going to keep it? Oh, I adore it, I really do. Thank you, Chance. At least I don't have to feed it!"

"Brooke, could we sit down a minute?"

"Sure," she said, frowning slightly at his suddenly serious tone.

Seated on the sofa, Chance picked up Brooke's hand and held it tightly between his. He took a deep breath before attempting to speak and then looked directly into Brooke's eyes.

"Brooke," he said, his voice hushed, "I really like my Santa statue and my socks, but the greatest gift I've had this Christmas is you and your love. As each day went by and then our nights together, I could feel my love for you growing. It's beyond description in its depth now. It's deep enough, solid enough to last a lifetime. Brooke, I don't want to give my Christmas present back. I want you with me forever."

"Chance, I . . ."

"Wait," he said, leaning toward the end of the sofa and taking a small blue velvet box from the pocket of his jacket.

"No, oh, no," Brooke whispered.

"I'm asking you to marry me, Brooke," Chance said, opening the box to reveal a heart-shaped diamond ring. "Will you be my wife, my love, my best friend? Will you marry me?"

Yes! Yes! Oh, dear heaven, yes! her mind screamed as unnoticed tears streamed down her cheeks. "No, I…can't," she said, a shuddering sob escaping her throat.

"Brooke, you said that you loved me!"

"I do! Oh, Chance. I love you very much, and I trust and believe in your love. You were so patient with me when I was filled with self-doubt, and because you were, I finally rid myself of it. I don't want to give my Christmas present back, either, but I have to. I can't marry you, Chance."

"Why not?" he said, his voice rising slightly. "There's nothing standing in our way anymore."

"Yes, there is. Something has happened."

"What are you talking about?" he said, gripping her shoulders. "What's happened?"

"It wasn't intentional," she said, her voice starting to tremble. "I'm sorry, Chance."

"I don't understand."

"I conceived your child, Chance, in Aspen."

"You're pregnant with my baby?" he said, getting to his feet and dropping the ring box on the sofa. "You can't possibly know that yet."

"Yes, I do. Maybe only another woman could understand, but it was a magical moment, a gentle message to my heart and soul. It's true, I know it is."

Brooke looked up at Chance through her tears and saw his features change as the reality of her words struck him to his inner core. His body went rigid, tight, and his jaw was clenched. A pulse beat in the strong column of his neck, and his hands were trembling as he curled them into tight fists at his sides.

"Damn you!" he roared. "What gave you the right to do this? That's our baby, Brooke, not just yours. That moment was mine, too. I'm surprised you even bothered to tell me."

"I wasn't going to! I didn't want you to feel responsible, but your grandfather convinced me that—"

"My grandfather knows about this?"

"Yes, I talked to him. He said you deserved to know about your own child."

"Mine? Hell, it isn't mine. Oh, I planted the seed in you like some kind of stud, but mine? No, Brooke. My baby is going to be planned, discussed, and I'm going to know when it's conceived. I won't find out about it as an afterthought. Damn it to hell, I can't believe this!"

"Chance, please try to understand. I didn't set out to get pregnant. You were there, you know how it all came to be. Chance, I love you! I didn't even know how important that moment was to you until it was too late. I didn't mean to hurt you. I want this baby, Chance, and I want to be your wife."

"Anything else?" he said, a bitter edge to his voice.

"Chance, please."

"And you had trouble trusting me at first? Guess what? I've got enough disbelief in you, who you are, what makes you tick, to last forever. You're a stranger, someone I don't know. This ball game is over because I'm blowing the final whistle myself. I'm finished. You'll hear from my attorney."

"Your attorney? Why?"

"Money, Brooke, for our... *your* baby. I'll see that you have everything you need."

"No! No, damn you, no! I won't take one cent from you. You said it, Chance. This baby is mine. We don't need you or your money. Your grandfather was wrong. I should never have told you. You're throwing a lifetime away for one moment, one little moment."

"Oh, now I'm the bad guy here? No way. Don't try to lay a guilt trip on me, Brooke. I'll financially provide for that child, but that's the only obligation I have. Damn! We could

have had everything. Ah, hell," he said, grabbing his jacket,
"I've had it."

"Where are you going?"

"Does it matter? It's over, Brooke. I can't handle this.
I've got nowhere to put it, no way to fix it in my head so I
can live with it. You took total control over something that
was half mine. Well, now it's all yours."

"Chance, wait!"

"Goodbye, Brooke. Enjoy your Christmas."

"Chance!" Brooke screamed.

But he was gone.

The loud slamming of the door caused Brooke to cover
her ears, and then she gave way to the tears that choked her.
She cried until she was exhausted and then pushed herself to
her feet and stumbled across the room, colliding with the
enormous Saint Bernard.

"Hi, dog," she sniffled, patting its black shiny nose.
"How's life? Keep smiling like that—maybe it will help. Oh,
dog, Chance is gone. Is Chance a cold, calculating, data-
finding computer genius like you'd think? No, he's so sentimental and romantic it's ridiculous. Dear, but ridiculous.
This situation is crazy, but I love him so much. I think I'll
have a hot fudge sundae."

The day was the worst series of hours Brooke had spent
in her entire life. She cleaned up the Christmas wrap and
placed Chance's Santa figurine carefully in the tissue in the
gold box. Together with his new pair of sweat socks, she
placed them in her dresser drawer. As she sank back onto
the sofa, her hand came to rest on the blue velvet box, and
the sight of the beautiful ring caused her to burst into tears
again. And so the day went. She alternated between crying,
talking to the Saint Bernard that she officially named Dog,
eating hot fudge sundaes and crying some more. She was so
sick to her stomach by nine o'clock that night from her

overindulgence of the sweet dessert that she flung herself across the bed and cried herself to sleep.

The next day Brooke mailed the ring to Chance. With tears running down her face, she accepted a tissue from a sympathetic postal employee and then hurried out of the post office. When the telephone rang at eight that night, Brooke mumbled her hello.

"Brooke?"

"Chance?"

"Yeah. How are you?"

"Was there something specfic you wanted?"

"A couple of things. I left my clothes and shaving kit over there, and I was wondering if I could stop by and pick them up."

"When?"

"Tonight? Half hour?"

"Fine. What else?"

"I, um, spoke with my attorney. When your...pregnancy can be confirmed by a doctor, I need a statement in writing."

"Stuff it, Tabor," she said and slammed the receiver into place.

When the telephone rang again a moment later, she snatched up the receiver.

"Now what?" she yelled.

"Hello, sunshine, nice mood you're in. This is Willie Tabor."

"Oh, Willie, I'm sorry. I thought it was Chance with more of his insults."

"That boy is in a world of hurt, honey. Even worse than I expected. You didn't even get to have your Christmas, did you?"

"No, Willie, we didn't. I—I can't talk about it without crying."

"Okay, honey. I just wanted you to know I'm here if you need a friend."

"Thank you, Willie. Good night."

A short time later Chance knocked quietly on the door, and Brooke jumped to her feet and pressed her hands to her cheeks. She counted slowly to ten and then answered the summons with her nose tilted in the air.

"Hello, Brooke," Chance said quietly. "May I come in?"

"Yes." She nodded, frowning as she saw the fatigue etched on his handsome face.

"You hung up on me," he said as she closed the door.

"You bet I did. I don't intend to accept one cent from you, Chance Tabor, let alone prove to your fancy attorney that I'm pregnant. You have a lot of nerve."

"Just how do you plan to provide for our...your child?"

"That doesn't concern you."

"The hell it doesn't!"

"Would you please collect your things and leave? I mailed the ring to you today, by the way."

"It's yours. I don't want it back."

"Return it to the jeweler."

"I'll get my stuff. Do you want me to take the Saint Bernard out of your way?"

"Dog? No! He's mine. I adore him."

"Whatever," he shrugged, heading for the bedroom. "You named him Dog? Dumb."

"I didn't ask your opinion."

"You didn't ask my opinion on a lot of things," he said, spinning around and glaring at her. "Like, for example, the subject of me becoming a father! Do you think it's a girl?"

"Well," she said, squinting at the ceiling, "it's either a girl...or a boy."

"Cute," he mumbled, disappearing into the bedroom and returning a few minutes later with his clothes rolled into a bundle.

"Goodbye," she said, looking at a spot on the far wall. "You're wrinkling your clothes."

"It doesn't matter. Well, take care of yourself."

"I will."

"Brooke, I . . . Good night."

"Good night," she whispered and managed not to cry until he was safely out the door.

The next night Chance called at seven.

"Brooke?"

"Yes."

"I forgot my shaving kit at your place. May I come and get it?"

"When?"

"Twenty minutes?"

"Okay," she sighed.

Brooke was eating a hot fudge sundae when Chance arrived, and she carried the bowl with her to answer the door.

"Hi. What is that? Hot fudge? Are you nuts?"

"No, I'm nervous. You upset me."

"Do you know what kind of preservatives are in that junk? Didn't you read the label?"

"I don't worry about that stuff. Heavens, there'd be nothing left to eat or drink if people took all that nonsense seriously."

"Nonsense? You can stand there poisoning your system knowing you're carrying my...our...*your* baby? Shame on you."

"You gave me a gallon of it!"

"That was before you were pregnant. I mean, before I knew you were pregnant. Do not eat another bite. And no coffee. None."

"Says who?" she yelled.

"Me!" he said, thumping his chest.

"Thirty seconds! That's what you have to get your shaving kit and get out of my house."

"You haven't heard the last of this," he said, stalking toward the bathroom. "Hello, Dog. You sure have a stupid name. She'll probably call the baby Baby."

"Out!" Brooke shrieked.

Brooke's mouth dropped open as Chance marched out of the bathroom and into the kitchen, reappearing with her jug of fudge sauce and the canister labeled sugar that contained her coffee.

"What are you doing?" she said none too quietly.

"You need a keeper, lady. This stuff is off-limits. Goodbye."

"That's stealing!"

"Call the cops!" he said and slammed the door behind him.

"The man is a lunatic! A bona fide crazy!"

Brooke was so glad to return to work the next day that she almost hugged her typewriter. She assured her boss that she'd had an absolutely marvelous Christmas and then rolled her eyes toward the heavens when Mr. Wilson walked away. Her day was busy, and she was grateful that there was little opportunity to think of Chance Tabor. Only about every three seconds or so.

The telephone was ringing when Brooke entered her apartment at six that evening.

"Brooke?"

"No."

"I forgot my gifts, my Santa and the socks."

"When do you want to come?" she said, tapping her foot.

"Fifteen minutes?"

"Right."

When Chance arrived, Brooke decided that he looked much better and had apparently gotten some sleep. Her heart did a tap dance beneath her breast as she caught the familiar aroma of his after-shave and drank in the sight of his wide shoulders in his sheepskin jacket. He was so beautiful, and she loved him so much.

"What's in the sack?" she said, suddenly snapping out of her semitrance.

"Milk, cottage cheese, fresh fruit," he said, walking into the kitchen.

"Why?"

"I looked it up in a book at the library. This is great stuff for pregnant women. Milk products and citrus are excellent."

"Well, thank you, Dr. Spock. Chance, you cannot come in here and tell me what I'm to eat."

"Sure I can," he said, grinning at her over the top of the refrigerator door. "I just did. Do you have my presents?"

"I'll get them," she said, stomping away.

Chance was holding the framed picture of her sitting on his lap when Brooke reentered the living room.

"That was quite a day," he said quietly.

"It seems like a long time ago."

"Yes. A lot has happened since then."

Brooke nodded her head silently.

"Brooke," he said, setting the frame back on the coffee table, "I have to go out of town tomorrow. If you need anything, I want you to call my grandfather."

"No."

"Damn it, yes! I'll have enough on my mind in Japan without worrying—"

"Japan. Why are you going to Japan?"

"They have some high-tech equipment over there I've been itching to get my hands on. All of a sudden they said come ahead so I'm going there to meet them. Will you call my grandfather if—"

"No."

"I'm going to wring your neck!"

"I'm not afraid of you, Chance Tabor."

"You would be if you knew the mood I was in!"

"Big deal," she said, raising her chin. "I'll turn Dog loose on you."

"Oh, good," Chance said, bursting into laughter. "I'll rest a lot easier knowing he's here to protect you."

Brooke smiled and looked at Chance, whose expression was immediately serious again. Their eyes met and held in a timeless moment, and Brooke felt the familiar ache of tears in her throat. It took every ounce of her strength to stand perfectly still, to not fling herself into Chance's arms and tell him a rush of words that she would love him forever. Love him, and their child and the life the three of them could share.

Chance cleared his throat roughly and drew a shuddering breath before attempting to speak.

"May I have my presents?" he asked.

"What? Oh, yes, here."

"I'll call you when I get back. Please, Brooke, phone my grandfather if you need anything."

"Yes. Yes, I will."

"Thank you."

"Chance, why are you doing this? You stole my fudge sauce and brought me cottage cheese."

"I don't know," he said, raking his hand through his hair. "I can't think straight. I'll get myself squared away while I'm in Japan. I guess I've been bothering you the last few days."

"I don't mind. How long will you be gone?"

"About a month."

"Oh," Brooke said, a wave of icy misery washing over her. "Well, have a nice time."

"Yeah. I'll ... see you."

"Yes."

How long they stood there gazing into each other's eyes, Brooke couldn't have said. It might have been seconds or minutes or an hour—she didn't know. Then Chance suddenly turned and left the apartment without another word.

The next evening Gran appeared at Brooke's door.

"Hi," Brooke said, "come in. I wasn't sure you were back. Did you have fun?"

"So-so. There weren't any men my age on the loose in Aspen."

"Gran, when did you start toting a drink in your hand when you go visiting?"

"Oh, this? It's for you. Homemade eggnog. Marvelous concoction for someone in your condition."

"My what?" Brooke said, sinking onto the sofa.

"The baby, silly girl."

"What!"

"I'm so excited. Here, drink this."

"How did you find out?"

"Oh, Chance called me. He said he had to go to Japan, and he asked me to look after you because you're using very poor judgment about what you're eating."

"He told you about the baby and then he had the nerve to say I have poor judgment! I'll kill him!"

"Why aren't you two married by now?"

"It's a long miserable story. Chance and I are finished, kaput, done."

"Then why do I have this eggnog in my hand?"

"Beats me." Brooke shrugged. "Chance is acting very strangely."

"Drink this! Chance sounded like a worried father-to-be."

"It's my baby, not his."

"Oh? They don't make babies like they used to? How's it done these days?"

"Gran, please. I'm a wreck, I need a hot fudge sundae and Chance took my gallon jug. The baby is mine, and I intend to raise it alone."

"We'll see. Is that monster supposed to be a Saint Bernard?"

"That's Dog. Chance gave it to me for Christmas. Sweet, huh? That's what I asked for when I sat on his lap."

"Do you love Chance, honey?"

"With every breath in my body."

"Drink your eggnog."

At precisely seven o'clock the next night, Joey Rather was standing in Brooke's living room with a carton of orange juice in one hand and a book on prenatal care in the other.

"He didn't," Brooke said, covering her eyes with her hand. "Tell me Chance didn't call you with the news flash of the year."

"Yep. Man, I think it's so great, Beebee. Wow, take a look at the size of that dog!"

"Did Mr. Tabor mention that he and I are no longer seeing each other?"

"No. He just said he was going to Japan and wanted me to check up on you. I'm supposed to frisk your cupboards for fudge sauce and coffee."

"He is a dead man!"

"Beebee, are you and Chance having problems?"

"Joey, it's over!"

"Could have fooled me, kid." He grinned. "That was one shook-up dude on the phone. How pregnant are we?"

"We?"

"Hey, I'm family, aren't I? I'm an uncle-to-be. Want this juice in the refrigerator?"

"I'll take it. Answer the phone while I have my nervous breakdown."

"The residence of Beebee Bradley," Joey said into the receiver. "Julie? Is that you?"

Brooke spun around and watched as Joey lowered his tall frame onto the sofa.

"Julie? Honey?" he said. "Why are you crying? Honey, talk to me."

"She's crying?" Brooke whispered, clutching the orange juice carton tightly in her hands. "What's wrong? Joey?"

"Yeah, I hear you," he said. "Slow down a bit. You what? What?"

"For Pete's sake, what's going on?" Brooke yelled.

"Shhh," Joey said, "she's very upset. Go ahead, honey. Yeah. You do? You're sure? Oh, Julie, of course I do. There's nothing to forgive. I love you so much."

"Ohhh, how nice," Brooke said, smiling.

"Listen to me," Joey said. "Don't move or breathe or think. I'm flying to L.A. tonight, and we're going straight to Vegas to get married. Okay? You will? Oh, Julie, I love you. I'm on my way. Oh, Julie? Beebee and Chance are pregnant. Bye, babe. See you soon."

"You're getting married?" Brooke said, squeezing the carton so hard that orange juice came squirting out the top, drenching her from head to toe. "Oh, no!"

"Beebee," Joey said, grabbing her by the upper arms, "Julie is miserable. She hates modeling, misses me day and night, and we're getting married as soon as I can get us to Vegas."

"That's wonderful, Joey. I'm so very happy for you both."

"Uh-oh. Here I am taking off and I promised Chance I'd watch over you."

"Go. I'll be fine."

"Love ya," he said, kissing her on the cheek. "You taste like orange juice. Bye."

"Bye," Brooke said, a lovely smile on her face.

The fact that Julie called back moments later did not surprise Brooke, and the two talked for the next hour. Julie had missed Joey so much that there had been no joy in her so-called glamorous career. Julie, of course, wanted to know what was going on with Brooke and Chance and was Brooke really pregnant? Brooke sniffled her way through the story.

"Oh, dear, what a mess," Julie said. "But if Chance is so blown away by what has happened, why did he ask Gran and Joey to look after you? I mean, the guy supposedly is dusting you off, right? It doesn't make sense."

"I know. He admitted he's mixed up but intends to straighten his head out while he's in Japan. I really don't think I'll ever see him again. He doesn't want this baby because of how it came to be. Oh, Julie, we were so close to having so much."

"Don't ever give up. Men are strange, wonderful creatures. Are you going to be all right there alone?"

"Yes, I'm fine. Go get married, Julie Mason. I love you and Joey dearly."

"Bye. I'll talk to you soon."

"Not too soon. You're going on your honeymoon! Good night, Julie."

When Brooke hung up the receiver, she became acutely aware that she was covered in sticky orange juice and headed for the shower, a wide smile on her face. She was thrilled for Julie and Joey, so very happy that it had all worked out for them and that they were to have a future together after all. Some people actually got a happy ending.

The following days fell into a routine. Brooke was extremely busy at the office, arrived home to receive her eggnog from Gran and spent the evenings thinking of Chance. Mac Bradley sent a hastily scribbled postcard saying that he had been delayed in Ireland and did not know when he would return. His Christmas gift of a pair of gaudy dangling earrings arrived and were stuffed in a dresser drawer.

When Julie and Joey returned to Denver, Brooke had a celebration dinner for them and invited Gran and, on impulse, Willie Tabor. Gran, bless her heart, flirted outrageously with Willie, who was captivated by the vivacious woman. It was a lovely party, a good time was had by all and Brooke thought about Chance.

Julie and Joey moved her belongings to his apartment, and Brooke promised to visit soon. The couple literally glowed with happiness, and Brooke thought about Chance.

One evening, when Brooke could no longer tolerate the lonely apartment, she went across the hall to see if Gran wanted to play gin rummy. Gran was preparing for a dinner date with Willie Tabor. Brooke shuffled home, had a nice loud cry, and ... thought about Chance.

But from Chance Tabor Brooke heard nothing.

It had been thirty-five days since Chance had left for Japan when Brooke went to the doctor. She had an evening appointment and arrived at the office after work.

"Well, Miss Bradley," the doctor said when they were seated in his office after the examination, "you came in here and told me you were pregnant and you are. About six weeks, I'd say."

"I can give you the exact date in December if you need it for your records."

"You had that little inner voice, huh?" He smiled. "Many women know the very minute they conceive. It's uncanny. Brooke, what about the father? Does he know?"

"Yes, but ..."

"He doesn't want this baby?"

"He did. I mean, he had it all planned—marriage, home, children. He loved me and wanted to share his life with me. But you see, Doctor, he had this thing about wanting to know when his child came to be. He's hurt, angry and ... well, the baby is mine now."

"He's throwing everything away over—"

"A precious moment. His life was all programmed and— That's it!" Brooke said, jumping to her feet. "Oh, why didn't I see this before!"

"What?"

"Chance gathered the data, ran it through his genius computer mind and produced a mental printout for his life. He's used to being in control, one step ahead of everything and everyone. For the first time there was a human element added. Me and my love. That was great until I did things out of order and goofed up the program. He doesn't know how to deal with that."

"You lost me back at gathering data, Brooke."

"Thank you, Doctor. This discussion has shown me so much. I'll see you in a month. Bye."

Brooke hurried home, her thoughts whirling. Suddenly everything became so clear.

Later that night Brooke talked to Willie Tabor on the telephone. Yes, Willie said, Chance had mapped out his career plans when he was fifteen years old, and everything was exactly on schedule. Willie also knew that Chance had been up-front in his relationships with women in the past, had set the ground rules, called the shots and ended them when he decided. His financial investments were carefully organized and all had returned hefty profits.

"Don't you see, Willie?" Brooke said. "Chance is a walking computer. Granted, he's warm and caring and dear, but, Willie, he is facing the one thing he can't program from first step to last—love. The printout wasn't followed and he's floundering, he's confused. He doesn't know how to regroup and start over because everything has always gone exactly as he calculated it."

"This is definitely making sense," Willie said thoughtfully. "I blame myself for some of this, honey. I've always been so proud of Chance, of the way his mind works, the things he's accomplished. I should have realized he was heading for a fall and it would happen when he fell in love. Trouble is, you got hurt right along with him."

"It's not your fault and it's not Chance's. His way has worked beautifully for him, and he had no reason not to believe that it always would."

"So? Now what?"

"Now, Willie? I'm going to fight for the man I love, the father of my baby. Chance may be a genius, but he's still got a few things to learn. Just pray I win."

"Honey, I'll be rooting for you every inch of the way. I suggest that you hit Chance with a board to get his attention first, though. He can be a very stubborn boy."

"I know. He's back from Japan and hasn't contacted me at all."

"But he isn't back. He got tied up longer than expected. He's due in tomorrow morning."

"Really? Well, we'll see what happens. Remember, Willie, don't breathe a word of this to Chance."

"My lips are sealed."

"How are things with you and Gran?"

"Dandy, just dandy. Virginia is a lovely lady, Brooke."

"Marvelous. Thank you for talking to me, Willie. You're a dear."

"Ho ho ho. Good luck, sweetheart. Give our boy hell."

When Brooke stepped off the elevator at six the next evening, she saw Chance Tabor leaning against her door. It took every ounce of her willpower not to run down the hallway and fling herself into his arms. She walked slowly toward him and smiled politely when she stopped in front of him.

"Hello, Chance," she said, praying that her voice was steady. "How was Japan?"

"Oriental. May I come in?"

"If you like," she said, inserting her key in the lock. Oh, he was beautiful! Tanned and tall, strong and . . . beautiful. His thick hair was curling up over his ears and collar because he needed a trim, and his blue eyes were sapphire pools. She loved him. Oh, dear heaven, how she did love this man! "Take off your coat and sit down," she said, shutting the door. "Did you hear the good news about Julie and Joey?"

"Yes, Joey had my address in Japan, and they sent me a telegram. I'm really happy for them," he said, shrugging out of his jacket and sitting on the sofa. "How are you, Brooke?"

"Fine," she said, hanging her coat in the closet and sitting on the opposite end of the sofa.

"Have you seen a doctor?"

"Oh, yes, and he confirmed my pregnancy. I did not, however, get a letter to that effect for your attorney."

"Forget about that. I know you're pregnant. I'll tell my lawyer to set up a fund for you."

"No, Chance. I won't accept your money. You didn't plan this baby, you don't want it and the responsibility is mine."

"Damn," he said, raking his hand through his hair, "you haven't given an inch since I've been gone."

"Have *you*?"

"I've thought about this a great deal in the past weeks. Brooke, I don't doubt for a minute that you'll be a good mother. It's this whole pregnancy bit that has me worried. You don't eat right, and you're working hard all day. You need looking after during these months. What if I hired a woman to move in here and cook and—"

"No! That's still taking your money."

"Well, damn it, do you have a better idea?"

"Let's see," she said, tapping her chin with her fingertip. "Do I have this straight? Once the baby arrives, you figure I'll do fine, but in the meantime I need a keeper."

"Not a keeper exactly, a . . ."

"Friend?"

"Yeah, a friend. Julie is busy with Joey, Gran is bonkers for my grandfather, according to him, and no one is free to devote their time to watching over you."

"Except you."

"What?"

"Are you already involved with another woman?"

"Of course not!"

"Well, then it's perfect. Chance, I'll rent Julie's room to you, which will help me financially without my feeling like a charity case. You'll be on the premises to see that I don't slip over the edge and eat forty-two hot fudge sundaes. Good plan, huh?"

"We'd be roommates?"

"Yes, and friends. I realize our romantic involvement is over. But I've hurt you enough without denying your request to free your mind of worrying during these months. It's the least I can do after my inexcusable behavior of getting pregnant without your knowledge. Yes, Chance, I will definitely do this for you. You should move in immediately."

Chance shook his head slightly as if trying to clear it and stared at Brooke.

"I'll wait," she said pleasantly, "while you compute all the data in your mind."

Chance got up and began to pace the floor in long, heavy strides. Brooke studied her fingernails, peered at Chance from beneath her lashes and forced herself not to tug on her curls. Chance finally halted his walking and stared down at her.

"All right," he said, "you've got a deal. I'll move in tomorrow."

Nine

Brooke managed not to let out a great sigh of relief until Chance had left the apartment. He'd appeared rather dazed when she had handed him a key and rattled on about there being plenty of closet and dresser space. Then she had patted him on the cheek, called him roomie and hustled him out the door.

That night Brooke had her first bout of morning sickness at 2:00 a.m. Weak and dizzy, she stumbled back to bed and huddled under the covers.

"That's all right, baby," she said, resting her hand on her stomach. "I don't always do things on schedule, either."

Brooke appeared pale the next morning, but her stomach was back to normal as she drove to work. It was a long day because she had mental visions of Chance changing his mind and refusing to move in to the apartment. Her fears were forgotten when she entered the living room at six to find him stretched out on the sofa. He had his nose buried in a book, and there were at least a dozen volumes on the coffee table.

"Hello," she said, "all moved in?"

"Yes."

"What are you doing?"

"Reading."

"I can see that."

"This is all stuff on pregnancy. There's diets, exercises, a book on names, everything. Are your breasts tender?"

"I beg your pardon?"

"According to this, your breasts should be slightly tender by now. Are they?"

"Well, yes, but . . ."

"Great. Has your waistline thickened at all?"

"Chance, for Pete's sake!"

"Don't you want to know what's happening to your body?"

"It's pregnant. I'll wait and be surprised about everything else."

"Very bad. We have to be prepared. I'll study this and make a projected report."

"Chance, this is a baby, not a computer program!"

"So? Data is data. First thing I'd better do is plan your meals. Oh, Gran brought your eggnog over. It's in the refrigerator. You know," he said, swinging around and sitting up, "you look terrible."

"Well, thanks a bunch!"

"Don't you feel well?"

"I'm just tired."

"You go lie down while I make dinner."

"Don't be silly. I'll relax after we eat."

"Brooke, go lie down!"

"Fine," she said, throwing up her hands. "Why not?"

Brooke changed into her fleecy robe, crawled between the sheets on the bed and fell instantly asleep.

"Brooke?"

"Hmmm?"

"You've been sleeping for an hour. Could you wake up and eat?"

"What? Oh, sure. I didn't realize I was so tired. I'll be right there."

Chance had already eaten but sat opposite her at the table and watched her consume her meal. His eyes followed the fork from the plate to her mouth to the plate again.

"You're driving me crazy, Chance." Brooke frowned. "Just what is your problem?"

"Nothing. I'm just making sure you eat enough. I think I'll chart and graph your weight gaining process."

"You certainly will not!"

"Why? It will be fascinating."

"Chance, I am a pregnant woman, not a floppy disk containing some information you've never been in contact with before. Don't you feel anything emotionally about this child?"

"We've covered all that. I was supposed to be aware of when it was conceived. It's as though that baby got there without any help from me."

"Remember sophomore biology? You are the father."

"Physically, yes. Emotionally, I don't picture that baby as being directly connected with me. I care about what happens to you, Brooke, that's why I'm here. I'll take care of you to the best of my ability but don't expect me to get all sentimental over that child. Go put your feet up. You have to watch for swelling."

Brooke opened her mouth to protest and then closed it again, shook her head and went into the living room. The battle before her was going to be even tougher than she had anticipated, she thought miserably. Chance had mentally crawled back inside his computer and refused to budge. The plan he had formulated in his mind as to how his life would flow once he fell in love had not come to pass. Instead of being willing to make a minor adjustment, he was chucking the whole thing, her and their baby included.

Somehow she had to make him understand that what they had wasn't over; it was just beginning. He had to weigh their future and that of their child. Life was *not* a printout from a cold, mechanical machine. Her love was warm and real and for eternity. Chance needed to listen to his heart instead of his head and add the human element back into his existence.

Could she teach Chance the beauty of welcoming each new day as a separate, glorious entity instead of mapping out his life the way he did? Could he learn to accept her as a woman, one who made mistakes but who never intentionally set out to hurt him? And the baby. Would he continue to denounce it simply because its conception did not follow his well-ordered plan? Would he, could he, come to love Brooke again?

"I don't know." Brooke sighed. "I just don't know."

"The kitchen is clean," Chance said, coming into the room and sitting down next to her. "Did the doctor say you were in good health?"

"Yes."

"What about diet? Vitamins?"

"I have all the information, Chance."

"This book says your hormones are kind of wacky so if you feel like crying, go right ahead."

"You're ever so kind," Brooke said, rolling her eyes.

"If you have any questions, just ask. I'll study every one of those books and memorize each little detail. We'll breeze right on through this thing."

"I think I'll go to bed."

"You just got up."

"I'm tired. Good night."

"Well, okay. Good night."

At exactly 2:00 a.m. Brooke ran to the bathroom and was violently sick to her stomach. She was so dizzy that she sat on the floor and rested her forehead on the cool rim of the tub.

"Brooke!" Chance said, pounding on the bathroom door. "What's wrong! Open up!"

"It's not locked," she said weakly.

"My God, Brooke," Chance said, dropping to one knee beside her, "what happened?"

"Morning sickness," she said, her eyes flickering over his massive bare chest, the dark, curly hair, the faded jeans low on his narrow hips.

"It's the middle of the night! You can't be sick now!"

"Maybe the baby forgot to read that chapter! Ohhh, I'm dying."

Chance scooped her into his arms and carried her back to bed, sitting down next to her after pulling up the blankets.

"You're so pale," he said, taking her hand between his two large ones. "I think I'd better call the doctor."

"No, Chance. Morning sickness is a very common ailment."

"It's the middle of the night!"

"You already said that! Not everything in life follows some preordained schedule. There are variables, you know."

"I don't like this. You really look awful. Why does morning sickness have to make you so sick? What can I do to make you feel better? Oh, honey, you're shivering. Body heat, that's what you need."

Before Brooke realized what he was doing, Chance had slid under the blankets and cradled her close to his chest. Her cheek was resting on the muscled wall, and the curly hair felt silky against her soft skin. Her senses were filled with Chance's special aroma, and she was acutely aware of his strength, the heat emanating from his rugged length. Her hand crept up to rest on his chest, and she could feel the steady beat of his heart beneath her palm. As she moved her fingers, they found his male nipple, and she heard his sharp intake of breath.

"Feeling... better?" he said, his voice slightly strained.

"A little," she said, desire swirling unchecked within her. "You can't be very comfortable in those jeans."

"I'm fine. Try to sleep."

Oh, sure, Brooke thought. Just nod off when she wanted this man to make love to her so badly that she was aching inside. Didn't he desire her anymore? Not at all?

Brooke wiggled restlessly and then a smile came to her lips as she felt Chance's arousal pressing against her through the material of his tight jeans and her flannel nightie. Oh, yes, Chance Tabor wanted her. Well, thank goodness for that much at least.

"Quit... squirming," he said.

"Sorry."

"How long have you been getting sick like this?"

"This is only the second night."

"I hate it! This has got to stop."

"Well, it will eventually."

"I mean now! I don't want you being sick, Brooke. Having a baby is supposed to be a special event, and it sure as hell shouldn't include landing on the bathroom floor in the middle of the night. Oh, man, what have I done to you?"

"Nothing! I did it, remember? *My* baby is upsetting my stomach. You're getting awfully emotional for someone who isn't emotionally involved here."

"I should have known you weren't using birth control. I knew you well enough by then to realize you hadn't let anyone near you since that joker who messed up your head. Where was my sense of responsibility in Aspen? Where was my brain? My logical reasoning?"

"Forgotten in the throes of passion!" Brooke said dramatically.

"Shhh, I'm thinking."

"I'm sleeping. Good night."

"This is driving me crazy, Brooke. There's something missing here that I can't figure out."

"Chance, please, go to sleep. I'm so tired."

"What? Oh, I'm sorry, babe. You just close your eyes and I'll hold you right here in my arms."

"Thank you, Chance," she said, snuggling closer and sliding her hand down to his waist.

"Stop . . . that."

"Pardon me?" she said, lifting her head to look at him.

"Ah, hell," he growled and claimed her mouth in a rough, searing kiss.

Hello, Chance Tabor, Brooke thought dreamily. Hello, hello, hello. Welcome home.

"Oh, Brooke. No, I've got to get out of this bed."

"I missed you, Chance. I missed you, I want you and I love you so very much."

"No, I can't. I just can't. I thought I had everything squared away in my mind, but all of a sudden I'm confused again. It wouldn't be right or fair to make love now. Man, my mind is oatmeal, total mush. I worked it all through while I was in Japan, and now I'm back to square one."

"All right, Chance. We'll just go to sleep. Night."

"What? Oh, yeah, good night," he said, shutting off the light.

Brooke smiled and closed her eyes. Chance was confused and that was fantastic. It meant there was hope that he might emerge from his dilemma and reach out his hand to her and their child. For Chance to be muddled, to not have a clear-cut picture of exactly what he was doing, must be extremely upsetting for him. He was questioning his actions and seemingly trying to get in touch with himself. And he was there, with her, close and warm.

The next morning Chance was not in a terrific mood.

"No way!" he roared. "You can't go to work. You were sick half the night."

"I'm fine. Stop yelling."

"Brooke, I want you to get back in that bed!"

"Is that a proposition, sir?" she said with a smile.

"It certainly is not! You need rest. Quit your job."

"What? Don't be ridiculous."

"I mean it. Quit your damned job!"

"This conversation is absurd. I'll see you tonight."

"Brooke!"

"Ta-ta," she said breezily, leaving the apartment.

The day was an uneventful one for Brooke, and she thought of Chance often. She was looking forward to seeing him that night. It seemed as if the day would never end, but five o'clock finally did roll around, and Brooke headed back to the apartment.

Chance was late getting home that evening and appeared tired when he entered the living room.

"Problems?" Brooke said.

"A computer was down and left us short of equipment so I had to wait until a machine was free."

"I saved you some dinner."

"No, thanks. I'm not very hungry. Brooke, there's something I think you should know."

"Oh?"

"I love you."

"You do?"

"Yeah. I didn't like you a whole helluva lot for a while there, but I never stopped loving you. I thought I had, but I realize now that my love for you was there all along. I guess that doesn't mean much at this point."

"Yes, it does, Chance. It means a great deal to me. I love you, too, and I trust and believe in you. I know it took me longer than it should have to realize you were real, sincere, but that was my inner flaw."

"Brooke, I—"

"No, please, hear me out. It was because of your patience and understanding that I came to have that trust, be able to believe in myself and then in you. What would you have me do? Go back to being who I was before? Throw up my hands and chalk you up as another example of my lousy judgment? Well, I refused to do that. I've conquered my insecurities, but I'm still human, I make mistakes, and when I do, I say I'm sorry. I'm sorry I conceived this child without your knowledge. I'm sorry I hurt you so badly. The fact remains that I do love you and want to spend the rest of my life with you.''

"You don't understand, do you?" Chance said, his jaw tightening. "You can't disturb the natural order of things and expect everything to be fine. That's not very realistic.''

"Natural order? Don't you mean the order that you decided things should happen? You alone, with no discussion with me. There are people in this world who would say we were wicked for having slept together without being married, but that was our choice to make.''

"Granted! And it was supposed to be our decision as to when we had a baby!''

"You, Mr. Tabor, aren't having it. I am! Oh, Chance, for once in your life can't you bend a little? Throw out the program you had in your mind and accept how things are. Line them all up again in their new order and take a good look at what you see. Is it really so different from what you ultimately wanted?''

"I spent the rest of last night realigning everything and it didn't work! You know why? There's a piece missing! There's a hole in the middle of the program, and I don't know what goes there.''

"Well, don't look at me! I didn't take it! I disrupted one moment of your life, and the roof caved in. I certainly won't make the same mistake again.''

"I—Brooke, will you be all right here alone?''

"Of course. Why?''

"I'm going out for a while. I just need to be by myself and sort things through.''

"But you haven't eaten.''

"Later maybe. I'll see you."

Brooke watched as Chance left the apartment, and then she wrapped her arms around herself, holding her elbows in a protective gesture. What she was doing to Chance was wrong, and the realization hit her so forcefully that she started to tremble. She was guilty of trying to program *him*. He had functioned in a certain manner all of his life, and she had decided to change that. Chance operated in a world of tight control and long-range detailed plans. Everything he did was organized and mistake free.

The turmoil he was now suffering was her fault. She was attempting to push his buttons, make him perform in the manner that *she* now prescribed. He was fighting with himself, was distressed, unhappy. She had to let him go, allow him to return to a world he understood. That place did not include unplanned babies and morning sickness in the middle of the night. Nor did it encompass a life with a woman who insisted that Chance change into someone he couldn't be.

She loved him. She loved Chance with every fiber of her being, but she had caused him nothing but grief. She would bid him . . . a gentle farewell.

Chance returned to the apartment shortly after midnight and frowned when he saw Brooke sitting on the sofa.

"You need your sleep," he said. "Why are you up?"

"I need to talk to you."

"Can't it wait? You should be in bed."

"It's important, Chance."

"Okay, go ahead, but talk fast."

"I've done you a terrible injustice."

"Again?"

"Yes," she sighed, "again."

"You're having twins?" he said with a grin.

"This isn't funny, Chance. I tried to change you into something you just can't be. I wanted you to accept a program different from the one you wrote, and your floppy disk rejected it.''

"That sounds sexy."

"Would you be serious? You are who you are, and that means everything happens just as you planned. I've seen how this pregnancy and my subsequent efforts to get you to accept this baby and me have made you unhappy. It's no good, Chance. It just isn't going to work for us. I'm very sorry I've caused you so much pain."

Chance looked at her with a rather polite expression on his face, and a silence fell over the room.

"Oh!" he said finally. "Is that it? Is your sermonette over?"

"Weren't you listening?"

"Yes. I caught every word. Well, it was nice chatting with you, but I'm beat. Catch ya later."

"Hold it!" Brooke yelled as Chance started to leave the room.

"You rang?"

"Did you hear me say that you and I together are a disaster?"

"Yeah, I heard that. Oh, by the way, you know that piece of the program I was missing?"

"Yes."

"I found it. Night."

"You what? Chance? Well, hell's bells, he went to bed!"

Brooke muttered her way through her preparations for bed and scowled as she crawled under the blankets. Chance had totally ignored her noble gesture, the baring of her soul. That was rude! The nerve of that man! He'd found the missing piece? Oh, whoop-de-do for him. So what was it, for Pete's sake? He at least could have told her. Now what was going to happen? He'd compute the data from her words and move out? Oh, she was just too tired to think about it anymore tonight.

When Brooke dashed from the bedroom at 2:00 a.m., she collided with Chance.

"Gangway!" she yelled.

"Good Lord," he mumbled, following close on her heels.

After Brooke had been terribly sick to her stomach, Chance gently washed her face, gave her a drink of water and carried her back to bed.

"I feel lousy," she sniffled. "Thank you for being here. Why are you up?"

"It was two o'clock and I thought you might need me," he said, sliding into bed next to her. "Go to sleep, Brooke. I'll hold you and I'll be right here."

"Ohhh, how sweet," she said and fell sound asleep.

The next morning Chance leaned against the door frame of Brooke's room, crossed his arms over his sweater-clad chest and frowned.

"You move out of that bed," he said, "and I'll break your toe."

"You wouldn't do that."

"Try me."

"But my boss—"

"I'll call him."

"Sold," Brooke said and closed her eyes.

When Brooke woke again at ten, she went in search of Chance but found only a note taped to the end of Dog's nose. It said, "Eat. Rest. I love you. C."

Brooke showered, shampooed her hair and dressed in jeans that were slightly snug around the waist and a fluffy pink sweater. Chance called at noon.

"Hi," he said. "How are you?"

"Fine. I feel very well."

"Great. Would you like to go out to dinner tonight? I realize you may regret your decision at two in the morning, but... Well, what do you think?"

"I'd love to."

"I'll pick you up at seven."

"That's tricky. You live here."

"No, this is a real date. I'll go to my apartment and change and officially pick you up."

"Whatever."

"Good. See ya."

"Chance?" Brooke said to the dial tone. They were going out on a date? Good grief, the man had slipped over the edge.

Brooke chose her dress carefully and decided on a pale blue wool outfit that fell to midcalf, nipped in at the waist and had tiny pearl buttons down the front. The prospect of the evening ahead held exciting appeal, and she firmly resolved to push aside all her distressing, confusing thoughts and thoroughly enjoy herself. She would be in the company of a devastatingly handsome man who was witty, charming and attentive, and she would simply enjoy.

Chance knocked at the door at precisely seven, and Brooke's mouth dropped open as he stepped into the room. He was wearing a perfectly tailored black suit and tie with a steel-gray silk shirt.

"You are absolutely beautiful," she said quietly.

"So are you," he said, pulling her into his arms and kissing her deeply.

Brooke melted against him and returned the kiss in total abandonment. Chance drew a ragged breath and then claimed her mouth again. Their tongues met and passions soared, and then he moved her gently away from him.

"We'd better go," he said.

"Yes. I'll get my coat. Did you lose your key?"

"No. I knocked because this is a date."

"Oh." She shrugged. "I guess that makes sense."

The night was clear and cold, and Chance turned on the heater in the car.

"Chance, are you going to explain about the missing piece to the program you found?"

"Yes."

"When?"

"Later."

"Did you pay any attention at all when I said you and I are a hopeless situation?"

"You spoke, I listened."

"And?"

"You're wrong."

"Oh? You'd consider ours a relationship made in heaven?"

"No, in Aspen."

"What do you mean?"

"I'll tell you later."

Brooke squinted warily when Julie and Joey miraculously appeared outside the restaurant at the exact moment that Chance helped Brooke out of the car. During the meal their conversation centered on friendly chitchat and various topics, and Chance even went so far as to order Brooke a hot fudge sundae for dessert.

"That's it for the duration," he said, "so enjoy every bite. Tomorrow it's back to eggnogs."

"Yuck," Brooke said.

"My, my, look at the time," Julie said. "It is just so very late and I must get to bed. Right, Joey? Let's go."

"Yes!" Joey said, unwinding his lanky frame and getting to his feet. "It was good to see you and—"

"Joey!" Julie said.

"We're gone," Joey said, grabbing Julie's arm and hustling her away.

"And what, pray tell," Brooke said, "was that all about?"

"Julie's tired, I guess."

"Oh, ha! You knew they were going to be here."

"Yeah, I set it up. I thought you deserved a quiet dinner with people who care about you. I ruined your Christmas, left you for a month and now you've been sick. I wanted you to have a nice time."

"I had a lovely time. Thank you, Chance."

"You may not thank me at two. You sure ate a lot."

"I was really hungry."

"We have to talk, Brooke."

"I know."

"That's another reason I'm your official date for the night. You can throw me out of your apartment any time you want to end the evening."

"Are we going home now?"

"Yes, I prefer to say what's on my mind in private."

"Am I going to cry, Chance?" she whispered.

"I wish I knew. Come on."

As each mile passed on the way back to Brooke's, Chance grew more tense. Brooke could literally feel him tighten up, saw the rigid set to his shoulders and the muscle twitching in his jaw. A wave of impending doom swept over her, and a knot tightened in her stomach. Her hot fudge sundae was dancing a jig, and she had the miserable thought that she would be early for her 2:00 a.m. rendezvous.

In the apartment Chance led her by the hand to the sofa and pushed her gently down by the shoulders. He pulled off his tie, stuffed it in his pocket and shrugged out of his jacket. He opened his mouth as if to speak, closed it again and paced the floor for several minutes. Brooke sat with her hands clutched tightly in her lap.

"Brooke," he said finally.

"What!" she yelled. "Oh, you scared me."

"Who else would be talking? Dog?"

"Sorry. You're just making me so nervous."

"Forget it, no more hot fudge. Brooke, I love you. I love you with every breath in my body. Do you believe that I love you?"

"Yes, Chance, I do."

"Good. That helps. I'm a louse, Brooke, a real sleaze ball."

"You are? What did you do?"

"Before I even met you, I had decided how my life would go when I fell in love. I had every detail worked out in my mind, and I was simply waiting for the right woman to pop onto the scene. Then there you were sitting on my lap asking me, well, Santa Claus, for a Saint Bernard. You and your nine freckles and soft curls knocked me over. You were everything I had ever hoped to find. The fact that you didn't trust me at first was just a minor setback, nothing I couldn't handle. I intended to marry you and live out the program just the way I had computed it in my mind."

"Then Aspen," Brooke said softly.

"Yeah, Aspen. Aspen and our baby. It's taken me this long to find the missing piece, to realize what I did. I swear, Brooke, I didn't know it at the time. It was buried so deeply in my subconscious and..."

"I don't understand."

"Brooke, I was scared to death. I couldn't get you to make a commitment to me further than being my Christmas present. I wanted, needed you with me forever, not just through the holidays. Oh, babe, I still find it hard to believe I could do something like that. My program was shot to hell and I was losing you. Nothing was going according to plan, and a part of me I didn't know existed took over."

"What are you talking about?"

"My flaw, Brooke. An inner flaw so big it makes the one you had the size of a grain of sand. My life was so programmed that I forgot, or never knew, how to be human with strengths and weaknesses and see and accept them in others. When you didn't follow the plan I had set up for my life, I couldn't handle it. I didn't know how to deal with it. I felt cornered and so damned scared. Fear causes a chilling ache and I fought you and the truth, and I hurt you so much."

"But..."

"Listen, okay? Do you have any idea what it's like for a man like me to realize he's totally lost it? I knew you weren't protected in Aspen, but I made love with you anyway. I've never done anything so irresponsible in my life. There I was, Mr. Wonderful, so caught up with wanting you, needing you, that I followed my heart instead of my mind. Me! Know where that put me, Brooke? Right in line with the bozos you'd chosen to trust in the past and had been wrong about. But you never gave up on me or your newfound belief in yourself."

"No. No, I didn't."

"It all piled up on me, blew my mind. Somehow I managed to bury it so deep within me it was as though none of it were true. I couldn't face myself because I didn't know who I was anymore. Do you want to throw me out now?"

"Not yet. Go on."

"What can I say? You know the rest. You got pregnant and I went crazy. Oh, Brooke, I'm so ashamed of my actions. I was being eaten alive by something I didn't understand so I took it out on you. I reverted all the way back to my program, claimed you had destroyed my dream and stolen the precious moment that my child was conceived. You didn't steal it, Brooke. I was there. I knew it was taking place just as you did."

"Oh, Chance," Brooke said, brushing a tear off her cheek.

"There aren't words to tell you how sorry I am. I'm begging you for your forgiveness. I took your gift, my present, and treated you so badly. Brooke, I love you and I love our baby. I want you both. I need you both. Ah, Brooke, please don't leave me alone to live out my life with computers and printouts. Marry me, Brooke, please!"

Brooke literally flung herself into Chance's arms as tears spilled onto her cheeks.

"Oh, Chance, I knew it! I just new there was more to you than computing data in your mind and producing a program for your life that had no room for human error. It took love to show you that, Chance. Love can't be plotted, it has to grow, blossom, like a beautiful flower. Each new facet of it is new and wonderful and full of surprises."

"I nearly destroyed our love, Brooke. For the first time in my life, I wasn't in control, couldn't push a button, state my plan and have everything go the way I worked it out. I understand now, I really do. I'm going to greet each day with you with a smile and wait to see what unfolds. Every moment with you will be precious, a gift. Will you, Brooke? Will you marry me?"

"Yes, Oh, yes, Chance."

"We'll be a family. You, me and our baby."

"And Dog."

"Speaking of that, I have something for you. I stole it from you and I want to give it back."

"What is it?"

"Your Merry Christmas. I behaved so badly that day. I bet I've been drummed out of the Santa Suit Society. Stay right here. Don't move. I'll be back in a flash."

"Where are you going?" Brooke asked as Chance went running out the apartment door. "He's bonkers, poor guy, but I love him so much."

"Ho ho ho!" a voice boomed.

And there in the doorway was . . . Santa Claus!

"Oh!" Brooke gasped.

"Ho ho ho, honey!"

"Willie? Is that you?"

"Ho ho yep! Mer-r-r-y Christmas!"

Willie entered the living room in his full red-suited attire with a huge sack in his hands. Chance and a smiling Gran were close behind, and Gran was carrying a tray of Christmas cookies.

"Merry Christmas, Brooke," Chance said, coming to Brooke and pulling her into his arms.

"Thank you, but how did you arrange all this?"

"They've been over at Gran's praying you'd agree to marry me. I wanted to make up for ruining your holiday.

We're going to have a lifetime of Christmases together now."

"Ho ho oops," Willie said. "This present is getting wiggly."

"Open the sack, Brooke," Chance said.

It was the fluffiest, cutest Saint Bernard puppy Brooke had ever seen. She laughed in delight as it shivered and shook and wagged its tail, and then licked her on the end of her nose.

"Hello, little puppy," she said smiling. "You are adorable. Oh, Chance, he's so darling."

"You like him?"

"Yes!"

"Think maybe we should get a house with a yard for him to play in?"

"Perfect."

"Ho ho ho and time to go back to the North Pole," Willie said. "Merry Christmas, children. Bless you both. This is a grand day in my life."

"And mine, too." Gran sniffled, hugging Brooke and Chance.

"Thank you both," Brooke said.

"Good night," Willie and Gran chorused as they left the apartment.

"They're wonderful," Brooke said, "and so are you. Merry Christmas, Chance."

He claimed her mouth in a soft, sensuous kiss that deepened immediately into a passionate embrace that sent their desires soaring. Chance lifted Brooke into his arms and carried her into the bedroom where he set her on her feet. As he reached for the blankets on the bed, his eyes widened as he saw the puppy sitting squarely on top of the pillow wagging his tail.

"Sorry, fella," Chance said, picking him up, "you weren't invited. I've got a nifty old sweatshirt you can sleep with in my room."

As Chance disappeared with the bundle of fur, Brooke hastily shed her clothing and then threw back the blankets. She turned to face Chance as he reentered the room, and he stopped, his eyes sweeping over her naked form.

"You're so beautiful," he said, coming slowly toward her. "My wife, the mother of my child. You are mine."

"Forever," she said, lifting her arms to receive him into her embrace. "I love you, Chance."

He kissed her, his hands sliding over her soft curves and pressing her to him to feel the announcement of his need for her. Chance lifted her onto the cool sheets and then stripped off his clothes before stretching out next to her. His hand rested on her stomach, and an expression of wonder and awe came to his face.

"Our baby," he said quietly. "Yours and mine. You, your love, this child, are the greatest gifts I have ever received."

"Merry Christmas, Chance," she whispered.

"And many, many more."

Chance lowered his lips to hers, and their tongues met in the sweet darkness of Brooke's mouth as his hand trailed over her dewy skin. Where his hand had been, his lips followed, kissing every inch of her lissome body. Brooke, too, conducted a lambent journey over Chance's rugged length, touching, kissing the steely muscles.

His mouth sought her breasts, and he drew first one, then the other bud into his mouth with gentleness, aware of the new tenderness. Heartbeats quickened as passions soared. Breathing became labored and echoed in the quiet room. But still they held back—postponing, anticipating the ecstasy of what they would share.

Chance claimed Brooke's mouth again, his tongue delving within as his hand slid to the heated core of her femininity. She arched her back to bring him closer, to seek, to find what she so desperately sought.

"Chance! Please!"

"Oh, yes, my Brooke."

He came to her with a thrust that took her breath away and swept her above time and space. It was a union like none before—a union speaking of commitment, understanding, love and forever. An instant later they burst upon the treasured place, calling to the other, clinging to each other as they slipped into oblivion. Together.

They drifted slowly back, then Chance shifted away and pulled Brooke to his side. She snuggled against him, relishing his heat, strength, inhaling his special scent. She was sated, contented and filled with immeasurable joy.

"Sleep," Chance said, kissing her on the forehead.

"For a while. I have an appointment at two, I suppose."

"Do you realize how organized our baby is? Right on time every night. That's brilliant, do you know that? That kid has this whole thing so carefully programmed that—"

"Chance!"

"Oh, sorry. Some old habits are hard to break, but I'll get a handle on it. Brooke? I love you."

"And I love you, my Santa Claus, and I will forever."

Months later Julie Virginia Tabor came into the world at 2:10 a.m. She had a headful of dark, curly hair and made her presence known with a lusty cry. Brooke smiled through her tears as the baby was placed on her stomach. And Chance? He missed the whole thing when he passed out cold in the delivery room and had to be carried out by two burly orderlies.

Later, in Brooke's room at the hospital, Chance kissed her deeply.

"Our daughter is sensational," he said. "She's gorgeous. Smart, too. She's got those nurses jumping in the nursery every time she squeaks."

"Chance, do you feel . . . Oh, I don't know . . . sad? You missed the precious moment of Julie Virginia's birth. Is that all right?"

"I can't believe I did that," he said frowning. "After all those months coaching you in those childbirth classes and splat! Right on the floor. There was a time when I'd be totally blown away because things didn't follow my program but not anymore. You taught me about loving, Brooke. You showed me how to live and love one day at a time. I missed Julie Virginia's birth, but I'll be right there to see her grow and blossom into a happy little girl."

"I'm glad. I was afraid you'd be upset. This calls for a celebration. Hot fudge sundaes!"

"You've got it. I'll order you a dozen. Ah, Brooke, I love you so much."

"I love you, too, my Chance. Do you think maybe when our second baby is born you'll try going into the delivery room again?"

"Brooke? Ho ho no!"

Their mingled laughter danced through the air, and then gentle smiles formed on their lips as they gazed into each other's eyes. Time would pass, the seasons would change one by one, but for Brooke and Chance every day would be like Christmas.

Silhouette Desire

Available
January 1987

NEVADA
SILVER

The third book in the exciting
Desire Trilogy by Joan Hohl.

The Sharp brothers are back, along with
sister Kit . . . and Logan McKittrick.

Kit's loved Logan all her life and, with a little
help from the silver glow of a Nevada night,
she must convince the stubborn rancher that
she's a woman who needs a man's love—not
the protection of another brother.

Don't miss *Nevada Silver*—Kit and
Logan's story and the conclusion
of Joan Hohl's acclaimed
Desire Trilogy.